MW01247209

LOVE & LIES
A SECRET MEMOIR

Ann Hymes

Secant Publishing
SALISBURY, MARYLAND

Secant Publishing, LLC
Salisbury MD 21801

www.secantpublishing.com

ISBN 978-1-944962-72-2 (hardcover)
ISBN 978-1-944962-70-8 (paperback)
ISBN 978-1-944962-71-5 (e-book)

Library of Congress Control Number: 2020904841

This novel is entirely a work of fiction. The names, characters, and incidents portrayed in it are the work of the author's imagination. Any resemblance to actual persons, living or dead, or to actual events is entirely coincidental.

BY ANN HYMES

Shadow of Whimsy: A Cape Cod Love Story

Love & Lies: A Secret Memoir

For Miss Dorothy Scroggie
and 9th grade English teachers everywhere

Chapter One

A woman can hide in the raising of sons. She knows the limits of their curiosity, the way their bodies charge ahead of their logic, and the risk in realizing that their masculine reflections may only mirror the reluctant image of their mothers. I know. I have been married for fifty years and had three sons not fathered by my husband.

The story begins almost forty years ago this summer, when I inherited Whimsy Towers, an oceanfront home in Chatham, Massachusetts. Clad in cedar shake and weathered by years of wind and storms, the house was where my southern grandmother had fled to escape an unhappy marriage. Leaving the strictures of South Carolina Lowcountry and a domineering husband, she first went abroad and tasted the Parisian life of the 1920s. Grandmother Theodosia was not much suited to conformity, and she came back pregnant with the child of a famous, and married, French artist.

Her displeased lawyer husband preferred deception to disclosure, saving face to admitting cuckoldry. While he probably wanted to display his adulterous wife on an old-fashioned cucking stool to bolster his own righteous superiority, he decided to turn a blind eye to indiscretion. His place in society provided armor from prying eyes, and position and prestige bolstered his resolve. Southern gentlemen of means determined the public face of the household, and Grandfather soon developed his own shadowy habits of illicit pleasure and intimacy. Women who were content to be in the orbit of his power did not question him, but Theodosia was not so pliant. She gave birth to their daughter, my mother, under the pretense of a prosperous and important family continuing their southern lineage, but she could not continue the charade.

How Theodosia Hampton came to Cape Cod is a mystery, and no one remains who can tell me. Her daughter, Emily, conceived in the passion of misspent freedom, was early sent to boarding school, with visits to her father in South Carolina and her mother on the Cape. The semblance of a family was maintained long-distance, with divorce not an option for a man who saw women as decoration and the necessary carrier for continuing the family name. Why Theodosia married him, I do not know, but expectations of the time may have weighed heavily on her heart, crushing her with duty.

The likelihood of continuing a loveless marriage was the tipping point for a free spirit who would not be caged, and she must have challenged and disappointed her husband in many ways. I have several letters from Grandfather to Theodosia after the Stock Market Crash of 1929. He was trying to hold onto his world, his wealth, his sense of order:

I see no way for you to remain in Cape Cod, and I will make temporary adjustments in my personal and social arrangements for your return to our house. It may be necessary to send Emily to a different school or to a non-boarding school when you are back in South Carolina. These changes need to be made to protect our family name and prospects.

Theodosia evidently did not respond well to folding her tents. She stayed put on Cape Cod. Now I am in her house and will tell you about the love and lies that have surrounded me, but first you need to know about Stormy.

All the movies and books and songs in the world cannot touch the love story of my grandmother and her seafaring lover. A fisherman, the captain of a small charter boat out of Provincetown, Massachusetts, he washed up on the shore of her life with the simple desire to be with her, to adore and value her. He was younger and shy, not schooled in the demands of society, which I think made him more attractive to the outgoing and beautiful Theodosia. I met Stormy as an old man, after my grandmother's death. She had left me her estate, including the house with bright pink trim and two towers that flash red and green colored beams far out into the ocean. I did not know Theodosia. I have had to recreate my grandmother in my mind. Sometimes now I cannot separate the prelude of another woman at Whimsy Towers from my time here. Our parallel lives might have touched, and sometimes I think I am living her life. I am the only child of her only child.

Like the rushing flow of streams that meet and blend, our stories share power that roils and carves its way through the landscape with dogged determination. There is urgency at Whimsy Towers. Families have crumbled and then risen from the ashes. I am part of that continuity; I feel its pull. We are women who could not stay put, who could not settle, who need passion and purpose. Some women dare to defy and can hold secrets without remorse; some cannot. Stormy was my link to a lost family. But I am meandering from the present and going too quickly into the past.

My attention must stay on track. I need to think about my son's funeral.

How do you say goodbye to your child? How do you admit to the wrong order of things?

ʘ

"I don't much take to puttin' people in the ground," Mattie said matter-of-factly, digging her hand deep into a bag of flour. Mattie had been spending the summers as housekeeper at Whimsy Towers for several years, since my sons found my car keys in the refrigerator at Thanksgiving. They saw erratic behavior in their aging mother, who was often alone at the ocean. I was safe here with my mistakes and my secrets, where dictates of conscience could hide in the corners.

"Ever since Mama rose up and scared the Jesus wits out of Pa, I been thinkin' it's not right to fill God's earth with boxes. They're not for growin'. Who decided that, anyway?"

I wasn't sure if Mattie was asking about my son David's upcoming burial arrangements or looking for worldly knowledge I might have collected, since cremation seemed to be the family way. Either way, I had sunk into sadness and grief, unable to converse about burial choices.

She continued without waiting for an answer. "You can't see God's face if you got walls down under." She paused, opening her fist to look at the clump of flour slipping through her black fingers, and then closed her eyes, singing in a low voice, *"No more walls, no more walls. Lord, Lord, no more walls...."*

Her hand sprinkled flour slowly across the dough board, as if her fingers moved on their own during this reverie. Mattie leaned into the counter and began to rub the flour around with both hands. She had made hundreds of biscuits on that board, with a rhythm that never varied. *"No more walls,"* she repeated, almost in a whisper, creating her own wall of silence and separation.

I couldn't tell if she wanted an answer or just time to reflect. Mattie was like that. She'd jump on an issue, ask questions and then think about it, drawing from the limited pool of her own experience. I watched her reach into the old green bowl that seemed always to have dough rising in it. Rolling and pounding flat the yeasty ball with her large, rough hands, she looked at me and asked seriously, "Do you want to be buried?"

I shuddered, tears forming. I frankly wondered how anyone could be committed to one place, in life or death. "No, no I don't. I want to be cremated and scattered." But David left no instruction. He had no opportunity to make a plan.

Whether Mattie wanted information on the history of underground burials, I do not know. I had little idea about evolving customs for the dead and was glad to leave the subject. I do know that people have been buried in caskets of honey and that John Paul Jones was initially laid to rest in straw and whiskey, but I realized later that Mattie was probably pursuing with me her own fears and choices, and I did not see it because of my own grief.

I'd heard the story of her mother several times. A frail and sickly woman, with a will to live and a body for dying, she had slipped away as the wretched hot summer in the South Carolina delta eased into fall. The family buried her near the shores of a quiet stream, where moss-draped trees arched over the grave. Fallen leaves covered the mound through winter months that barely cooled the sultry air. Mattie remembered these details of the place but had no idea where it was. There were tears and fainting and picnics with baskets of fried chicken and pies piled high with fruit, but the memories had wandered and lay in her head like exhausted nomads.

When spring arrived and the rains came, Mattie and her father did not visit the grave. For weeks it poured.

LOVE & LIES | 7

"Like heaven had to empty out," she used to tell me. But finally the skies cleared, and the soggy earth allowed father and daughter to walk the long road. The sweet, moist fragrance of jasmine surrounded them. Picking their way around dusty potholes turned to puddles, they swatted at flies and sang in low voices about God's mercy and care. Gospel songs unfolded heaven's plan, gathering the uncertainties of this life into a gift for the unknown. She'd never seen a chariot but knew with certainty that one was coming for her. She trusted the hand that held hers. At this point in the story, Mattie stopped and closed her eyes. What is horror to a child of five or six can continue to make its way in painful detail with the passage of time.

Before she knew why, her father had dropped her hand and run the last short distance to the grave. Her bare feet stuck in the mud, and she lost her balance without her father's hand to steady her. Half crawling, she stumbled toward the figure ahead, trying to see what had caused him to leave her.

There was her father, a big man, strong and stoic, collapsed in a heap of heaving sobs. His head dropped forward from his shoulders farther than any prayer had ever sent it. This man who didn't question God was wailing, "Why? Why?" As frightened Mattie slowly made her way toward him, she saw the exposed top of the plain wooden box that held her mother.

Bright yellow plastic flowers were scattered in the mud; some had slid toward the riverbank. She stood stunned. "I ... I got my dress dirty," she stuttered. When her father turned and saw her, he scooped up his daughter in his arms and silently made his way back home, never stopping to put her down.

"I was too scared to speak," she'd say. "I was afraid God was tryin' to send Mama back. I wondered if she'd been naughty; and if I was naughty, would God send me back someday."

Mattie never returned to the gravesite. As she thought about it years later, she assumed family and friends went back and moved the casket to higher ground. Within days, her God-fearing father took up alcohol and drowned himself within. "The devil's in the drink," Mattie would say, and she never in her life has touched a drop.

Chapter Two

My name is Theresa Alston Crandall. 1980 is the year that changed my life. I ventured from my home in northern Virginia to spend a few weeks on Cape Cod at Whimsy Towers, to explore a sudden inheritance and family history that turned everything upside down. My husband Kevin, steady and predictable, wanted to accompany me but knew I had to step into the unknown alone. Our marriage had lost its footing and was operating on cruise control. The future was uncertain. I was tempted to cast him off, like the wrapper of a candy I'd already eaten.

I was not an experienced traveler. I came to the Cape at age thirty-four, anxious for adventure, freedom, and the chance to explore possibilities outside the routine I knew so well. I was not expecting to find love or be unfaithful to my husband.

Raised by a widowed father who kept me close, I had basked in his attentive care and the safety of his love. Kevin was a version of my father, but dependable did not satisfy my growing restlessness. I yearned for the days when we had made love on the Oriental carpets and ate ice cream in the rain. We had been college sweethearts who made the plunge into matrimony with the optimism of youth. We loved each other with the naive hope that commitment would soften the rough edges, but our marriage evolved into patterns and habit. Routine crushes passion.

Now my body has long since lost its desire. Quickened breath is related to too many stairs. I do not wonder about the touch of a man's hand exploring my body. I dread the thought of anyone even seeing my softened flesh, which hangs in ways gravity has pulled it. I do not feel the need for sexual intimacy at all. My body is dead to desire, and Kevin's cannot rise to the challenge. Old age is one bookend of life, a relentless despot whose cold, dark face stares without blinking. Comfort and calm have replaced urgency in the bedroom. Raising a family added more sleep to nights of lovemaking.

We have settled into that place of familiarity that keeps us together without stress, without fear. Anticipation is the hope of waking to a new day. Sometimes I need a cane to steady my resolve.

I have always loved Kevin, but he has been an unsuspecting partner in the orchestrated façade of our life together. A good husband is a cushion for falling, a man who knows when to step in and when to hold back. Perhaps a good husband is not too inquisitive. My love for him has sheltered a lie, and I have often wondered if my wish to protect my husband has been fair to my sons and fair to another man who would be hauled in by casting my net over the past. You will learn the unraveling. Deception lies in wait of good intentions.

I arrived at Whimsy Towers in the spring of 1980, ready to reorganize my life at age thirty-four. A medical diagnosis had dashed our hopes of being able ever to bring a baby full term. I had miscarried. Our bodies just did not want to cooperate. As I think of it now, perhaps my marital unhappiness was depression, a mental state that withdrew from reality and wanted to create a fantasy from rainbows and wishbones. I certainly had nothing to complain about—a caring husband, a good provider, a beautiful home in Alexandria, and a career that allowed me to write and draw. My deceased grandmother shook our world with the house she left me and made me face choices that I had tried to avoid.

So how did we raise a family? That's the beginning of my secrets.

cs

Picture a large, weathered, two-story Cape Cod house, with an inviting porch and rolling lawn to the biggest expanse of blue water that your eyes can grasp. Picture the sun rising each morning out of that glistening, wet surface, sprinkled with dazzling bits of orange and yellow that melt with the emerging day. Then picture a young woman with a love of swimming naked, who is lonely and curious and eager for adventure. A woman who is bored with her life sees possibilities in others'.

I settled easily into Whimsy Towers with my yellow Labrador Gypsy. I swam and read and dug into the history of my family. I knew that my parents had moved in with Theodosia after college, and I was born on the Cape. But when I was two, my mother was lost in a sailing accident. She was an expert sailor but could not outwit or outrun a terrible storm that caught her too far out in the ocean. She was never found.

And so my life in Virginia began when my father moved me far from the scene of painful memories and Theodosia's deteriorating mental state. She was overcome with grief. She had lost her only child, the seed sown in her rebellious Parisian interlude, the joyful evidence of her independence from the husband still in South Carolina. Life just emptied out when Emily disappeared. Theodosia got a full-time nurse, and my father and I got a fresh start. I have no memories of Whimsy Towers or of the two women who lived here before me, but I'm in their space. I breathe the salt air that both filled and caressed their bodies and dashed their hopes. My father washed Whimsy Towers from my young mind. And now I, too, have lost a grown child. I feel the presence of Theodosia. I feel her emptiness. Something in a mother dies with the death of her child.

With a start, suddenly I was reminded that there was still a telephone landline in the house. "Hello?"

"Theresa, you didn't answer your cell phone. How are you holding up?" Kevin didn't wait for an answer. There is no possible good news two days after your child's death. "I've been on the phone with the funeral people today, and we settled the music. They've been very helpful."

It's their business to be helpful, I thought, but said nothing.

"Theresa, I'll be up tomorrow morning. We can go over the details. The notice for the service went out today."

Kevin is good at plans, at process. Lawyers know how to move along an issue. He is a good lawyer and a good father. He has been a good husband, too, though it took me years to settle into the rhythm of it. He's been trying to withdraw from his law firm, testing the waters of retirement by spending more time with me at the Cape this summer. His youngest child's passing was not an anticipated detour; he had just returned to Virginia the day before the accident.

"Have you heard from Tim? He's been trying to reach you."

"No, I'm sorry. I haven't ...." I replied.

I repeated the order of my sons' names to myself. I'd had three children in four years—three boys: Tim, Kevin Jr., and David. I think they often felt like triplets. Despite their differences, friends sometimes expected them to be like cookie-cutter duplicates. And now my baby is gone. My thirty-three-year-old baby.

"I'll call Tim, I promise."

"He's really worried about you."

"I'll call."

"I'll see you tomorrow, Theresa. Need anything from here?"

"No, no thanks," I responded, sounding aimless and lost even to myself.

I settled back into the cushy, striped sofa in the kitchen, a long-ago replacement for the flowery one that

Theodosia had left. A thirty-foot kitchen with cherubs and boats painted on the ceiling and furniture arranged in front of a large, stone fireplace created a welcoming, all-purpose room. I knew that Theodosia had often invited friends and artists to share her home. She and Stormy were the nucleus of a family that they invented.

He spent many evenings spread out on the furniture, looking so at ease in my home that he knew so well, telling me stories about his life with my grandmother. I often felt like an intruder in Theodosia's world, a visitor who came and forgot to leave. I had the keys to her house, but Stormy had the keys to her heart. He belonged where I did not. Their love blossomed and thrived in the sharing of it. Whimsy Towers was where creativity and friendship flourished, and gloom was not admitted. No wonder Grandfather never visited!

At first I mostly came for the summers with the children, leaving Kevin in Virginia to practice law and work long hours without guilt. Gradually, as the boys grew and Kevin took more time off, we have welcomed Virginia friends and friends of the boys'. Whimsy Towers has arms that stretch out in colored beams from the towers into the ocean at night, beckoning those who are lost or guiding those on their way; and Whimsy Towers has an open door that always has room for one more at the table, even a gathering of mourners.

"Do you want sea clam cakes with the sandwiches?" Mattie asked. "The caterers are tryin' to finalize the numbers."

How does one count the guests of grief? There is no RSVP to a funeral, no way to mark the calendar ahead, no way to count the outpouring of disbelief and shock. A healthy young man is not supposed to die.

"Yes to clam cakes, and we'll tell them the number tomorrow, when Mr. Kevin arrives."

Leaning on another is a skill I've had to develop; it did not come naturally. My father raised me with the encouragement to express myself and think independently. Is it possible to be our honest selves in a relationship? A motherless child has voids to fill.

I am torn between wanting to be close and needing space. Communication takes work. I am absent and present in one body, living in duality. Sometimes I cannot finish a sentence because getting to the end requires remembering how it began. I am holding on to strands of normalcy that occasionally slip away. Lapses are infrequent, but I fear what may tumble from my lips.

Carefully, I pushed the automatic dial on my cell phone. "Hello, Tim, honey. Are you on your way soon? Dad is coming up tomorrow morning, so you should probably come directly here. How's Elizabeth?"

There was a silence. Then my oldest child shared a familiar and dreaded response about his wife. "She's drunk. I don't think she can travel." His voice had the slightest hint of a southern accent, after living for years in South Carolina.

That very first summer at Whimsy Towers, I had met a young father and his two little girls, Katie and Elizabeth, on a whale-watching trip. Jeff had brought his children on vacation far from their alcoholic mother in South Carolina. He was a devoted and worried husband, a caring father, and a man who wanted a vacation from turmoil. We talked and laughed and looked like a family. When I returned the next summer with baby Timmy, Jeff and the girls were back, and Elizabeth loved helping me with diapers and bathing and baby entertainment. She doted on Tim. She wanted to push his stroller without help—or interference.

As the years went on, our families spent time together in Cape Cod, even holidays outside of summer at Whimsy Towers. Two more baby boys arrived with me, but Elizabeth continued to focus on Tim. She took walks with him, taught him how to ride a bicycle, and hugged him until he screamed. Her own mother was rarely able to function as a parent and mostly stayed in South Carolina in the company of bourbon. I think Elizabeth was developing her own maternal instincts and then romantic ones. Possessiveness is not a healthy addition to any relationship, but Elizabeth was fun and thoughtful and could beat Tim at tennis. She developed into a beautiful, if aggressive, young woman. We enjoyed her company, her good manners, and the southern drawl that made all the world feel more gracious and at ease.

Can you guess?

At the end of the summer just before Tim was headed to college at the University of Virginia, Elizabeth announced that she was pregnant. She was as calm with this news as if she would drop it and head out to the movies. Tim admitted to spending time with her inside our boathouse, afternoons and even all night. Boys can be awkward liars, but he had friends in Chatham that came and went during the summer, and he spent odd hours at their homes and in the boathouse. Or so I thought.

When this sexual relationship began, they would not tell us, but she must have gotten pregnant the first week they laid eyes on each other that year. Close friends have a familiarity that can slip into something more, and Tim was flattered and smitten—and clueless. He followed the desire of his body for hers, like a willing puppet that is powerless to deviate from the script.

Kevin and I were beyond distraught, confronting the ruin of Tim's future because of his inability to control his impulses—or to prevent pregnancy. He did not have a serious girlfriend at high school in Virginia, but he knew about consequences. Elizabeth was working on the Cape for the summer and nearly finished with college. Her stunned father broke down into tears, feeling the failure of his role as a father as well as a husband. I guess we all stumble over the empty promises that life will meet our needs and follow a path that we choose, but life has no guarantees. We plan, we hope, we whistle in the wind.

I was in no position to be shocked.

"What are you going to do? We really want you to come."

"I don't like leaving Liz."

"Would she be all right on her own?"

"I'm not sure." His beautiful wife had become an echo of her mother, drinking until she passed out. She and

Tim married four months into the pregnancy, and he had moved to South Carolina to work for Jeff, attending the local college at night. By Christmas, the heartbeat of the unborn baby had stopped, and they faced the new year as a couple thrown together without the prospect of a family, without the impetus that had forced them together. Elizabeth began to drink with her mother, shutting out the men who not only loved them but mourned for their marriages.

Tim isn't one for wishes. He took in stride what life provided, letting details find their place in the grander scheme of things. Creating another child, however, was not going to happen until his wife was sober. Almost twenty years have passed. She has tried and failed and tried again, but she was not strong enough to fight the enemy that wanted to defeat her.

My oldest son is rarely in touch with me and shares very little, but he has admitted that other opportunities for sexual intimacy have surfaced over the years, without his seeking them. He is still naïve about the wiles of a woman determined to have her way. He is a handsome, polite man, who works hard and doesn't look for trouble, but his kind nature is a magnet for hungry women. I think he keeps repeating that youthful summer in Cape Cod, being drawn to the arms that want him. But I am not a good example for being able to say No.

His smile is exactly like the man's who fathered him. Seeing my boys move into their thirties has reinforced their origins in my past with visual imprint. Their biological father was that age when they were conceived,

and they have grown into his image in many ways—
some subtle and some not. I must stay on guard. I must
stay on guard.

What Tim said next surprised me. "Mother, what
would you think if I brought someone else?"

"What kind of 'someone else'? Like a date to your
brother's funeral?"

"Well, if Liz cannot travel, her father will stay here to
watch her and not come up. I could bring a friend for
company."

"'Company'? Is that what you call it in the 21st century? Tim, our family has a history of infidelity. It is not
a topic off-limits."

"What? Who are you talking about? Do you mean
your unconventional grandmother?"

I had been too much in my own thoughts. My child
was dead. I tried to regain my composure and stammered something about Theodosia and her conceiving
my mother out of wedlock and my grandfather's parade
of women through his bedroom. I was anxious to shift
my meaning to another generation.

"Mother, there is no parade here. And I live with Elizabeth, remember? She shares my bed and still has hold
on my heart. We do the best we can, but it is not a marriage that works."

What *is* a marriage that works? It is the question that
haunted me as I ventured off to Cape Cod by myself so
many years ago. I struggled with the answer until I gave
in to desire and the compromise of secrets with content-
ment. I believe I created a marriage that works.

Successful marriage is the satisfaction of the parties, and grounding in truth was not a requirement.

"Bring her," I replied. "Bring her, and we will be glad to see you both."

Chapter Three

I am in no position to judge. It is easier to turn the mirror in other directions to avoid the hard look of facing one's self. Can I fairly assess my own behavior? Life is just different degrees of possibility. I have always loved adventure and risk. As a child, I climbed high in swinging treetops and jumped fences meant to stop me.

I am comfortable with pretending, which probably has led me to write and illustrate stories for children. I wonder if the world of make-believe has worse odds for success than the higher moral ground.

I've always felt the freedom to stumble and grow, to find my own voice. There was no competition for my father's attention and no sibling comparisons.

"No two cookies are the same," my father once said softly, biting into a large chocolate chip cookie from those we had just pulled from the oven. "The chips are always scattered differently." I took it as approval, but maybe it was acceptance.

I have always loved the potential of my life, but relationships with men are harder for women without broken wings.

Some women question their lives, and some do not. Some women subdue what they value in themselves to promote harmony. Some stay under the radar of conflict to avoid chaos. Women are afraid to disturb tranquility. I am in awe of Theodosia for her bravery in the 1920s.

I am now close to the age of Theodosia when she died, was found drowned at Whimsy Towers. Reality had lost its grip, and she wandered out in the night with a small silver cup to empty the ocean in search of her lost daughter. With difficulty, Stormy had shared the story with me, assuming his beloved Theodosia had been trying to beat the odds. She did not easily accept defeat. On most days, she no longer even knew who Stormy was, but he stayed with her and tried to protect her from the darkening shadows that arrived with each day. I can only imagine such a love.

She had been a strong and stubborn woman, unwilling to be suffocated by her marriage or society. She battled the demons of dementia and finally lost. Am I following her?

Theodosia was a fighter, and Stormy was a man lost without her. He died the second summer I came to Chatham, but he had lived to see Timmy and rest in the hope that Theodosia's house would carry on in our family.

ॐ

Rain began to fall. I heard wind pushing branches gently against the side of the house, scraping and squeaking. Mattie moved through rooms to close windows, blocking the wonderful breezes that roll up from the ocean but carry rain into the house. I've always loved rain. Upstairs it pounds on the large, domed skylight that nearly covers the garden room ceiling, where heavy drops gather in clumps that drip down the sides in zigzag patterns.

Years ago I installed a large brick patio next to the house, where I can step outside under an awning that is cranked out to cover the patio furniture and an area big enough for parties and a band. I often nap on the lounge. Soft floral cushions with bright pink and red flowers mirror the colors of the plants in big concrete pots. It is heavenly to be swallowed up by cushions. Surely heaven is the firmament of angels, a state of mind that welcomes and soothes, where thoughts are safe and forgiven.

"Hi, Mom," a familiar voice sounded from the hall. "Where are you?"

Mattie walked in with my middle son, Kevin Jr. As he came to hug me, she asked where I'd like lunch served. I felt his arms around me and I clung to him, trying to memorize the feel of him, and trying not to cry. Finally, I said, "Kev can help me outside. Let's eat with the raindrops under the awning."

"I'm so sorry I couldn't get here sooner, Mom. How are you doing? What can I do to help?"

Kev has always been a bundle of energy. He has never shown middle child insecurities or recriminations. He's a multi-tasker at home in the busy kitchen at The Lobster Pot in Provincetown, where he is a chef. The beginnings of a relationship between Stormy and my grandmother were nurtured in the back room of The Lobster Pot decades ago, where the foundation for love came from the friendship of opposites.

"Is Brad with you?" I asked my son, who has a serious partner.

"No, he's on the early shift but will come later."

The two of them together in the kitchen is a marvel to behold. They cut and slice and season and stir, moving around each other with the rhythm of dancers. They feel each other's movement and create a shared space. They have talked of marriage but feel no urgency.

"Mother, what are the plans? What can I do? I just can't believe it."

I felt tears welling up and waited a moment to greet or resist them. Rain slid down the slate roof onto the awning and fell in swollen drops off the edge, hitting the resistance of bricks. I could not hold the tears. They came with the slow momentum that builds to uncontrolled sobbing. I sat in silent sorrow, inconsolable.

I think sons are more affectionate toward their mothers than daughters. I have never felt the Oedipus complex in our household or seen any deviant behavior, but all my boys are huggers. When they began to practice their hugging skills on romantic partners varied with each one. A hug is the gateway to more. I think we are afraid of our bodies, guilty about the desires that come, afraid of false moves and fear of rejection. Sometimes we don't know what is missing until the unanticipated arrives.

"Thanks for coming, Kev," I managed to say at last. He had kneeled by my chair and was holding my hands in his. "Dad has made most of the arrangements, and he'll be here tomorrow morning. I don't suppose it's ever really possible to be ready, to be prepared. We'll have folks come here after the service. And I hope you'll approve of the caterers!" I endeavored to lift the mood but could not quite convince myself.

Kevin Jr. picked up the lapse. "I'll leave my cleavers at home," he said dryly, with a smile. "I'm sure they'll be fine."

Much about Whimsy Towers has remained the same over time. There is comfort and security in surroundings that resist change. When I look at the large Oriental carpet in the kitchen, I see my boys riding their tricycles over the patterned vases and our dog Gypsy snoring happily next to the woven birds that would always elude her. My head is filled with remembering. Long afternoons of making illicit love, rolling across the carpet with no regard for interruption or reprisal, lost in exploration and desire, life at Grandmother's house has met the needs of the moment.

I'm sure at least one of my boys must have been conceived on that carpet. It would be fun to think that Kev, with his love of cooking, had his beginning on the kitchen floor; but by then his father was not so reckless, and I dare not joke aloud. Kevin did not roll on carpets at Whimsy Towers. Unconventional lovemaking with Kevin gradually evolved into taking off each other's clothes as we fell onto the bed before the traditional routine. The youthful hunger we'd felt for each other tempered after we were diagnosed with the inability to carry a child. In a way, we clung to each other in grief, coming together physically to seal the stability of our marriage, to reinforce the guarantee of our survival. I loved Kevin. I have always loved him and known that he loved me, but it was not always enough.

Years ago we lost an unborn child, and now we mourn the loss of a living one. I have not seen my husband since the accident, have not had to face him or explain details. You see, I was there. I try hard to grasp the events, but fogginess engulfs the scene. I hear screaming and the screeching of metal; people are everywhere, too close and too loud. I am held by strangers and carried. It is dark. I can no longer see David.

On the phone, Kevin has tried not to add to our unspeakable grief. He is no less devastated, but he is a patient man, willing to postpone facts until they can be couched in careful conversation. The outcome will not change. Our son is not coming back. The circumstances and shock remain to be sorted out. What I remember is arguing, arguing with David about love.

"Kev, let's play Bananagrams before lunch," I suggested. "Where did I leave it?" I needed to give my mind a break from sadness, from the burden of lost memory.

My family humor me with playing. The game with lettered tiles provides an opportunity to create words and then pull them apart, to organize and reorganize the inventory of letters. It's like my mental process; nothing is quite fixed. Unlike Scrabble, the words have no value and are only a collection of possibilities until all the tiles are used up.

Bananagrams has no secret moves; nothing is hidden from the other player who is creating his own challenge.

Gradually the interlocking words creep across the table, like crossword puzzles of their own making.

"Great," said Kev, exasperated, as he looked at his 21 tiles. "I've drawn a V, a J, a Z, and two Cs. Not a promising start."

I carefully put all my vowels on one side, seeing what difficult consonants I could use up first with them. I had a V, a K, two Ls, and a Q, but no U. My new favorite word was QUA, an easy way to get rid of a Q. But with no U, I "dumped" the Q for three new tiles. We each moved our tiles around, forming and un-forming words. I soon used up all my tiles and called "Peel," the signal for us each to draw another letter. Kev was glad for reinforcement for his stragglers, but I quickly placed my tile and called "Peel" again.

While up to five or six can play the game, drawing fewer tiles to begin, I often play by myself and have gotten pretty good. Even small mental prowess is a victory these days. With some inner excitement, I pulled several words apart to create DEVASTATION, which also opened up places to add letters for new words. I silently congratulated myself for successful strategy and evidence of cohesive thinking—and called "Peel."

Mattie arrived with lunch of salad and sliced ham. She had made biscuits and strawberry jam, and Kev was quick to praise her. He knows a genuine southern biscuit. Your passion is not necessarily your talent, but Kevin Jr. has found a career that combines them and a partner that appreciates him. Of my three children, the middle one, often destined for dysfunction, has created a life of satisfaction and purpose. He introduced the man he was to the man he wanted to become. Perhaps we are always coming of age, finding new layers of life.

Kev wanted to be a better person. Simply responding to daily circumstances does not dig into our deficiencies but merely reshuffles the deck of daily duties. He turned his considerable energies into the pursuit of a better life. I often envied him. Matching our behavior with our values is not an easy peace to reach.

Kevin Jr. has set the bar high for those of us who have struggled to find our authentic selves and slipped, not always regaining our footing. At age thirty-five, he has a solid grip on his life. His world is not mine, but his tribe is a community of people connected to each other by acceptance and trust.

Conformity is punishment for my son whose moral compass spun out of control when he was younger. He followed his father's footsteps after college and went on to law school, dutifully excelling academically and imprudently experimenting personally. In 1987 I had seen the magnificent AIDS Memorial Quilt in Washington, D.C., spread out across the National Mall on a sunny day in the city of lawmaking—almost 2,000 panels of remembrance. It was a breathless reminder of lost lives and lost potential, a cruel reminder of society's indifference and intolerance.

Twenty years later, when my own child declared openly that he was gay, I knew it was not a choice but a mandate. He had to follow his own path and listen to the drummer that beckoned. He left the law, the pretense of societal inclinations and expectation, and refocused on finding what worked for him. As a mother, I feared for his personal safety and hoped that he had the strength to discern wisdom from whim.

We cannot hold on to the gift of these children. They stretch and grow and develop their wings. And then they fly away.

Family is the collection of people we are given. We cannot choose or stop the blood that flows through generations, but we choose our connections, not determined by blood or lineage. I often wonder how my sons would feel if they knew they have no physical connection to their father, who loves them unconditionally. And, of course, I wonder how my husband would feel. Is there forgiveness for good intentions? Can mistaken deeds offer recompense for empty lives? Infidelity completed our family, chasing away the possibility of going our separate ways.

And have I cheated their biological father by withholding their paternity or merely eliminated awkwardness and regret?

Kevin and I had explored the possibility of adoption after twelve years of marriage and no option of conceiving our own child. He was unwilling at first and then embraced the idea, probably to help save our marriage. We were both overjoyed when I realized I was pregnant not long after my first trip to Whimsy Towers. We accepted this minor miracle as a readjustment of our bodies for conception, and the pregnancy proceeded easily. We seemed to have defied the medical profession, the curse of incompatible blood types. Though we had made love before and after my few weeks away, I was certain whose seed had been sown, and it was not my husband's.

Chapter Four

The rain had slowed, and the air was moist and fragrant, with hints of honeysuckle, persistent and impatient. Large pots just outside the patio held plants that were leaning over from the cleansing rain that rinsed their leaves. Blue, red, and yellow flowers blended together in wild arrangements that had been told to live together; blushing tall grasses reached for the cloudy sky, and pink and white petunias cascaded over the edges. Herbs, annuals, and springtime bulbs shared space not logical for any gardener except David. He was my creative child. He loved to decorate, to beautify. It broke my heart to realize that the large floral arrangement on the dining room table was the last one he would ever do for us. He could not know that he was also making it for visitors to enjoy who would come to say goodbye.

A wide path of bricks laid in herringbone pattern leads to the rose gardens and maze of boxwood at Whimsy Towers. I have heirloom roses and modern varieties—red and yellow and pink—some with powerful scents and some that just strut their beauty. I really do not even like roses; they are fussy and demanding.

I had the maze installed as a game when the children were little and I was making up reasons for a local landscape gardener to come to the house. It began with miniature lilacs, a row of intoxicating, perfumed bushes next to the screened porch, and grew into flower beds, and coffee, an innocent look or touch, and then rides on the lawn mower, and attraction that soon left innocence behind.

"Mother. Mother, would you like to take a rest? I think you are wandering off somewhere," Kev said kindly, putting his hand on my shoulder.

"Oh, I'm sorry. I was just thinking about David and his flowers...and the gardens...and ...."

"Do you want to talk more about him, Mom? Tim and I understand and are not threatened or hurt by your feelings. We've been on the phone sharing our thoughts. We boys have lived separate lives, but we certainly know how deep your loss is and that there's probably no way to recover from losing a child. And David was your baby."

My baby.

I took a deep breath of misty air and gazed absently toward the ocean. "Would you and Brad like to have children?" I asked my surprised son, who was clearly expecting the conversation to go in a different direction. "Do you see yourself as a parent?"

"No disrespect, but I'd rather chew jalapeños. I can't imagine the sacrifice that having children requires. I think I'm too selfish. I love my life with Brad, and sharing it sounds like adding complexity with no expiration date. And never mind the cost, the education, the worry—and the wrecked cars!"

"Well, I understand the wrecked cars part. Boys seem to drop transmissions and drive up telephone poles and get stuck in wet fields with girls and beer, but I cannot imagine my life without you. We waited and hoped, wishing for a family. And curiosity is a strong motivator! I was an only child; I wanted to see siblings that shared or fought or whatever siblings do. Without a mother, I didn't really know how to be one, but children haven't taken the course, either. With each child, we got more relaxed. I can't imagine if we'd had to switch gears and raise a daughter."

Kev continued, "Since we were all born in the spring, I guess you and dad had high alert fertility months!" He laughed, and I tried to join in, without bringing too much to the observation that I always got pregnant in the summer.

"Seriously, Brad and I have talked about it. He would love to have kids, and he's hoping I'll soften up. He'd be a great father. We have friends who just had twins with a surrogate, which is a really frightening advertisement for parenthood. They're exhausted and wonder what happened to their life. Another couple have adopted a little boy. I'm not sure about schools in Provincetown."

"Dearest Kev, you'd be a terrific parent. Your work schedule is crazy, but you are patient and fun and have a willing partner. I think it's a positive sign that you are thinking about schools. I see you with a string of little girls with pink tutus and purple hair. And Dad and I could babysit. We'd love some children around. Between us, I think we could be a responsible party."

I realize the limits of my own abilities, occasionally having mental lapses that I cannot anticipate. I also fear for the future of Whimsy Towers without another generation coming along. Will Theodosia's house slip from the fingers of her family?

My boys all know that their father and I had trouble getting pregnant, but after a dozen years, the babies came in quick succession. Now fertility drugs have opened new possibilities for parenting, and same-sex couples have legal options—for themselves as well as for having children. David was my only son who was anxious to have a family, and his story was cut short. It was a Greek tragedy that could not have ended well, but I am getting ahead of myself. Secrets need their time.

When life is shattered and something you love is taken away, where do you go to regain balance, to see purpose in life? Though I love the Bible and can get lost in its grand literature, I have no religious tradition. And I'm afraid to lean too heavily on my husband, for fear of unloading my burden. In grieving the dead, I could devastate the living.

I am finding solace in poetry. Sometimes I cannot remember whether or not I have flossed my teeth or locked the door; but, oddly, my mind is remembering verses learned as far back as the eighth grade. Sometimes whole poems appear that wrap around me and lift me to their absent reality. I am safe with silent words. The metaphors and subtlety of shared imagination allow me to escape the present. I cannot bear the loss of my child, and I cannot remember the events of that day. What really happened?

Sometimes our daily lives act like a shell to keep us safe from truth. We see what is projected by others, and we make assumptions without knowledge. In turn, we project what we choose. The truth of a thing may not be evident.

"Richard Cory" by Edwin Arlington Robinson was one of the first poems that really got my attention. It was easy to memorize, with the simple rhyming and iambic pentameter. The reader is lulled along, until the startling end:

> *Whenever Richard Cory went down town,*
> *We people on the pavement looked at him:*
> *He was a gentleman from sole to crown,*
> *Clean favored and imperially slim.*
>
> *And he was always quietly arrayed,*
> *And he was always human when he talked,*
> *But still he fluttered pulses when he said,*
> *"Good-morning," and he glittered when he walked.*
>
> *And he was rich—yes, richer than a king—*
> *And admirably schooled in every grace:*
> *In fine, we thought that he was everything*
> *To make us wish that we were in his place.*
>
> *So on we worked, and waited for the light,*
> *And went without the meat and cursed the bread;*

> *And Richard Cory, one calm summer night,*
> *Went home and put a bullet through his head.*

We can be tricked and trick others, but we cannot trick ourselves forever.

I've been living on a pedestal, like Richard Cory. I've deceived *"the people on the pavement,"* hoping no one will notice my burden.

℅

"Kev, can you stay for supper?"

"Absolutely. I'm here until Dad arrives. I'm your watchdog and bodyguard, your chauffeur and helper. I can lay a table, clean a closet, tidy the porch, or read you poetry."

"What a lovely idea. Go tell Mattie, and then maybe we can read some 'Sonnets from the Portuguese.'" The book was a gift from my father when I graduated from high school. "Elizabeth Barrett Browning knew about life and love and loss." As Kev left the room, I began to read aloud from the slim volume in my lap:

> *I lift my heavy heart up solemnly,*
> *As once Electra her sepulchral urn,*
> *And, looking in thine eyes, I overturn*
> *The ashes at thy feet. Behold and see*
> *What a great heap of grief lay hid in me,*
> *And how the red wild sparkles dimly burn*
> *Through the ashen greyness. If thy foot in scorn*

Could tread them out to darkness utterly,
It might be well perhaps. But if instead
Thou wait beside me for the wind to blow
The grey dust up...those laurels on thine head,
O my Beloved, will not shield thee so,
That none of all the fires shall scorch and shred
The hair beneath. Stand farther off then! go!

When I finished, Kev took a few minutes to shuffle through the small book. "I'm tempted to read the familiar '*How do I love thee? Let me count the ways,*' but I think we're looking for new ground to cover. Is this getting too sad for you, Mother?"

"No, these are love poems, initially private thoughts about courtship and marriage, but they speak of universal themes. Loving doesn't require just one specific object. I'm glad to hear others' expressions of fear, of bereavement, of hope. Death is absence, but not defeat."

"Okay, but maybe we can finish with this one and then go out for an outing. It's too beautiful outdoors to stay inside all day. The rain has stopped and left a sunny afternoon, and we could use some cheering. Deal?"

"Deal."

Kevin Jr. has a voice for the stage, clear and strong. He and Brad work with the local theater in Provincetown, both in acting and mentoring young actors. In high school and college, he balanced academics with theater. Perhaps that's how he learned to juggle two worlds. Kev does not need the limelight; he needs to be part of a story. He can reach deep into a text to set the mood, delivering a message from printed words that have no power of their own without expression. I love to hear him read. He began:

> I see thine image through my tears tonight,
> And yet today I saw thee smiling. How
> Refer the cause? —Beloved, is it thou
> Or I, who makes me sad? The acolyte
> Amid the chanted joy and thankful rite
> May so fall flat, with pale insensate brow,
> On the altar-stair. I hear thy voice and vow,
> Perplexed, uncertain, since thou art out of sight,
> As he, in his swooning ears, the choir's amen.
> Beloved, dost thou love? Or did I see all
> The glory as I dreamed, and fainted when
> Too vehement light dilated my ideal,
> For my soul's eyes? Will that light come again,
> As now these tears come—falling hot and real?

We sat quietly for several moments, digesting both the apprehension and the eagerness of the poet. She was on the cusp of love; I am on the precipice. Do our expectations and hopes exceed the earthly possibilities? The uncertainties of life are reminders that we are not in control. To live is to lose.

Kev found the keys to my car, a Volvo C70 that is a hardtop convertible, and helped me down the few outside steps. I had first come to Whimsy Towers with a shiny new red Jeep and an aging yellow Lab; they are both now long gone. Nothing stays put.

I miss having a dog, a steady companion that just wants to please. Labs are like that. She let the children climb all over her but lived to see only two little boys who could share her as a pillow on the floor. She died in Virginia, but I brought her ashes here, to remain where she swam with waves that carried her with the ease that her legs could not.

"Kev, do you still have that cat you found behind the theater?"

"Oh, yes; rather, she still has us. She's an independent thing, which is good and bad. She lets us know when we humans may cross the line to pet or hold her. I suppose that being on her own created a wariness and independence. When her guard is down, she grants permission to pet her, and she purrs and purrs."

"Sounds like good preparation for parenting to me! When to step in and when to back off is the choreography of parents. Timing is the key, but the only insight comes from hindsight. I was often at a loss and look back in awe at how it all unfolded."

I think boys are not as devious as girls, as quick to blame. They are more willing to confide, and girls are more likely to keep secrets. It used to be that parents helped their children fit into society and the culture that nurtured them. Now children fight the culture of tradition and seek to navigate their own way. Boys stumble; girls plot.

"Dad and I have been so lucky. So very lucky ... until now."

"Mom, you and Dad did a great job. Seems to me that boys aren't as interested in rejecting their parents as girls are. High school was an especially difficult time for sorting out relationships, but the good news is that we generally live through it. And I suppose there is sweet revenge for parents when their children have children!"

"You are my philosopher child. I think because you worked so hard to deal with complex issues in your own life, you have a more generous view of others'."

"There is patience in self-doubt. I was in no position to judge anyone else when I couldn't figure out my own way, to see the honesty in my choices. There is hope in struggle. Brad often teases me about following the light at the end of the proverbial tunnel. I love you, Mom. You and Dad have always been such an example of devotion and loyalty."

I silently cringed at my son's words, and then congratulated myself that I, too, am a credible actor. My role as wife was chosen, my role as mother was a gift, my role as secret lover was a surprise. The play has had various acts, but without the final curtain. Soon I will tell you.

Chapter Five

"Shall we put the top down?" Kev asked.

"Absolutely," I replied, anxious for the sun on my face and wind in my hair. A convertible is perfect for the summers here. I never wear a hat, never care if I look tousled and untamed. While I still feel comfortable driving, I am glad to be driven. I fear the possibility of losing my license, of losing my independence. One slip of judgment or careless inattention, and I could harm myself or someone else. At my age, one mistake and I would not likely get a second.

"Let's sit a minute in front of the lighthouse," I suggested, as we navigated the long driveway to the road. The lighthouse is between Whimsy Towers and the little downtown, which is just a few blocks of shops designed for tourists. It is only a short walk into town, but I am no longer able to do it. Serious shopping and groceries are available further out, with unappealing parking lots and store names without novelty. Chatham is a town that knows the balance between those who visit and those who have roots. Even after almost four decades, I am still a guest from Virginia, a transient presence in Theodosia's house. Both her daughter and her granddaughter left her behind in Cape Cod, neither choosing to do it.

Do we find or create a sense of belonging? Is it a place or an attitude? I believe that home must be the deepest yearning inside us all.

Kev pulled into the assigned parking in front of the lighthouse, facing the broad expanse of sand giving way to the ocean. The repetition of repeating waves rolling onto the beach was soothing and hypnotic. Children and families ran along the edge of the water, yelling and waving, punctuating the calm of a sunny afternoon. I tried to picture my mother alone out in that vast ocean, fighting against a storm that quickly overtook a day that began safe for sailing. I closed my eyes, and the horror of her death was once again recreated on the silver screen of my imagination.

"Mother, would you like to get out for a minute?"

"Yes, let's have a stretch and then get an ice cream," I responded, coming back to the present. Kevin Jr. has the patience of Job, like his father, and offered me a steady arm to lean on as I got out of the car. We stood huddled against the wind, softly buffeted by salt air, memory, and the fragility of life. I wondered how I could ever let go of David.

"Rum raisin or strawberry?" Kev asked, stirring me from my absent musings. "I think this is a two-scoop kind of day."

I have always been ready for ice cream at any time, but mid-afternoon was perfect as a bridge between organized meals. We sat outside on a bench and tried to stay ahead of our melting cones, watching passersby with shopping bags and well-behaved dogs on leashes.

Arm in arm, we wandered into shops that offered imported leather goods, sundresses, and cardigan sweaters with appliquéd designs. Window displays enticed us with colorful arrangements of jewelry in gold with diamonds and gemstones. I have some stunning jewelry with diamonds and sapphires that had been my grandmother's, but I rarely wear it. It lives at the bank, safe from carelessness.

The stores were full of shoppers, and though I was getting tired, I felt glad to be spending time with my busy son. Kev is swept up in the pace of his own life, and I am someone to visit when there is time, when guilt pulls time forward. He slows his mental engines to accommodate me, and he is sincere, but I know he is only partly present; his brother's death has brought him to my side. Kev is a good son, duty-driven, but only David was really in my life, perhaps because he lived nearby in Washington, D.C. The other two sons are memories that check in.

While Kev looked at men's jackets, I sorted through blouses and hats and briefly thought of buying something new for David's funeral. And then I realized that I wanted to stay with what was old and comfortable and familiar—like wearing something he would recognize me in.

As we stepped outside and began heading back to the car, a man came up behind us, calling, "Excuse me. Excuse me!" We turned and saw him approaching with quickened step. "Excuse me," he said again, louder. "I'm afraid I need to look in your handbag."

"What?" I said, uncertain he was actually talking to me. Several women on the sidewalk stopped to listen, turning their backs discreetly, as if shielding a secret.

"What are you talking about?" echoed Kev.

"I'm sorry, but I need to see in your handbag. I'm a security guard, and we can do this here or at the police station."

"Are you from Mark, Fore, and Strike?" I asked, not offering my bag.

"Ma'am, they've been gone for many years. Could I please see your bag?"

Kev tightened his grip on me and motioned to give the man my handbag. Reluctantly, I offered up the bag, and the man rummaged inside. He lifted out two pairs of gloves that had price tags dangling conspicuously.

"Mother, what ....?" Kev looked totally at a loss.

"Ma'am, I'm afraid I need to detain you for shoplift-ing. Can you account for these gloves?"

"Yes, I have gloves," I replied, digging into my hand-bag and producing yet another pair of gloves, similar but worn.

"I'm afraid we need to continue this at the station. You'll need to come with me."

"Wait," interrupted my confused son. "May I bring her?"

"I have no problem with that. Just show me some identification first. Are you local?"

"My mother has lived here for decades. Surely there is some accommodation you can make. She sometimes gets confused and is hardly a shoplifter."

The security guard paused. "Just a minute. Wait here." He returned to the store, and the ladies who had gathered on the sidewalk shifted their huddle. The air was still, thick with the premonition of doom. Kev was speechless. We stood frozen in place, like players on a chessboard, waiting for the next move.

The nameless man returned, still holding the gloves. "The manager has told me to let you go. She will not press charges, with the provision that you do not return to this store."

"Thank you, sir," Kev said to the man who was about his own age. "We'll be more careful, and I appreciate your help with this. I assure you there was no devious intent."

"Intent or not, shoplifting is serious." And then he added, looking straight at my son, "You need to keep an eye on her."

The sidewalk ladies dispersed, whispering in low voices; the show was over. I had a momentary vision of Kev putting a collar and leash on me to guide me back to the car. I needed to sit down. I couldn't quite process the severity of the situation. There were too many gloves in my bag.

"Mom, do you understand what just happened?" Kev asked. "Why did you pick up those gloves?"

"I left my gloves on the table," I answered matter-of-factly. "I have a lot of gloves."

"But, Mom, you took gloves that were not yours."

"That man was nice to return them to me."

Kev looked up with a worried look I had never seen before. We walked slowly back to the car, silently. I was deep in thought about gloves that came and went and carried the possibility of a changed future.

"I think I need to rest a bit," I said as we pulled up to the house. "We've had quite a day."

Kev did not respond. I cannot know his thoughts, but as I lay on the lounge on the screened porch, I could hear him talking outside. Mattie was in the kitchen, so Kev was talking on his phone to someone else. His muffled words escaped me. And then sleep carried me off to a place that did not judge or ask questions.

When I awoke, Kev and Brad were playing backgammon on the table near me. It's a quiet game, with only the clink of dice hitting the board. No outbursts or challenges—a game for thinkers, with a roll of the dice for luck and direction. I used to love the strategy of it but now cannot always see the logic of the moves. I need too much time to maintain the train of thought and am no longer a worthy competitor.

They had moved a vase of flowers from the table to make room and had placed it on the side table next to me. Perhaps the powerful fragrance drew me from sleep.

David had mixed wildflowers with roses, marigolds and mint. For him, fresh flowers were part of the décor, not needing a special occasion. Things beautiful were a necessity, not a luxury. Flowers belonged. I wondered how long I would leave the floral arrangements he had left around the house. Dead flowers are ghoulish, but dead children leave footprints.

"Hello, Brad. Can you stay for dinner?" I asked, rousing.

"Yes, thanks, I'm staying all night, and Kev and I are helping Mattie with something special for dinner. He wants to try a new dish at the restaurant, and you will be the guinea pig."

"I am always an eager volunteer," I answered. "Kev is incapable of producing even mediocre food."

"I agree," said Brad, his broad grin aimed at the man he loved and who loved him back. Their hands briefly touched across the backgammon board, and they shared that moment of wonder between two people who are at ease with each other.

I was glad not to wake to talk of missing gloves. As I was wondering if Kev would mention it, Mattie stepped out into the porch with a tray of glasses of sweet tea. Bringing her special brew of southern iced tea had made believers of us all, and several varieties of mint grow with abandon in the garden here.

"I'll be working on an apple stack cake for awhile now, if nobody needs me," Mattie said, putting down the tray. "I want it to have plenty of time for restin.' You cannot hurry a stack cake."

Mattie is a purist, and she even peels, pares, and dries the apples for her special occasion cake, a recipe handed down through generations of her South Carolina family. I have watched her make apple stack cake, a tall, rough stack of layers made with buttermilk, sorghum syrup, dark brown sugar, and ground mace, as well as regular flour, salt, sugar, eggs, soda, and butter. It is labor-intensive, with each layer rolled into a ball and then flattened to cook one at a time in a cast-iron skillet liberally greased with shortening and then floured. The layers come out of the oven like huge cookies, reaching to the edge of the skillet; they do not rise like regular cake layers. The trick of the cake is to add the apple filling to each layer while it is warm. The top is left bare, to be sprinkled at the end with powdered sugar. When the cake cools completely, Mattie wraps it in cheesecloth and then several layers of plastic wrap. It sits on the counter for two or three days to "ripen," safely protected from eager forks and fingers. In my bedroom in Virginia, I have an antique pie safe, a tall, golden mellow piece of pine furniture with pierced tin sides that was once used for storing baked goods and now holds my sweaters. I like the thought that an entire piece of furniture was devoted to the safekeeping of such labors of love.

Mattie's cake will have five layers, always one for each member of our family. I wonder if her future cakes will have just four.

Kev handed me a glass of tea and announced his idea for dinner. "I was thinking of doing grilled halibut with a lobster-avocado appetizer. I'm experimenting with grilled or blackened halibut with leek-cauliflower mash and tomato-onion confit. Maybe baby kale to set off the color. What do you think?"

"I think that sounds wonderful, and I like the fish either way," I answered. "What a feast. I'm sorry your father will miss it."

"Well, Brad and I will still be here tomorrow, and I thought I'd do sea scallops baked in herb butter with a panko-parmesan crust. I know Dad likes scallops."

"Mattie will be sad to see you go!" I laughed, raising my glass in a mock toast to my son.

"She is doing desserts, and food is something I can contribute. Sometimes grief stokes the appetite."

Kev had arrived with what seemed a truckload of food. He appeared ready for any contingency. "Lobster with diced avocado and mango, with a special vinaigrette and herb-flavored mayonnaise, is something easy to put together at short notice," he continued. "As a matter of fact, let's try some now. I'm starving. With the size of your kitchen, there's room for an army to cook all at once; but I'll keep out of Mattie's way, or she'll have me slicing apples!"

Kev left the porch, and I turned to Brad. "I'm so glad to see you, and I'm sorry it's such a sad occasion. I consider you part of this family, and I'm grateful for your support and for your devotion to Kev. You seem like the perfect couple. I know how much he cares for you."

Brad did not speak. He took a sip of tea and then nervously poked down the ice cubes with a tall silver spoon. Mint leaves floated to the top. "We've been talking about having children," he said, slowly stirring the ice cubes. "It's a big step and a big decision."

"Yes, Kev told me. He said you would be a terrific father."

"The thing is, I've heard of an opportunity to adopt a baby boy. His mother is an opioid addict, and the father is unknown, a random choice on a bad night. The mother has relinquished him to the state, and I have a friend who is in a position to place him. I had just heard of this when we got the news about David. I haven't said anything yet to Kev. I'm not sure what to do. I don't want to add to his emotional load, but they need to know. And I need to know if he could love a child that is not biologically his own. Do you think that would be hard to do?"

Chapter Six

Can I not outrun my past? "Hard to do" is living a lie, but I cannot answer his question. I am not the parent whose genes have no influence on my children. Their father has been devoted and involved from the first inkling of their life, from the joy of kicking in my belly to sorting out issues of manhood. Kevin never allowed the expression "boys will be boys." He instilled the need for respectful behavior and demanded language to match it. For him there has never been a double standard. My husband has moral clarity.

He does not know that I have lived a double standard for all these years. I want desperately to believe that he would still love his sons with the same ardor, but I have usurped his option. I have hidden in deceit, not willing to unmask the lie, not willing to confess to infidelity. Kevin has unknowingly adopted another man's sons.

I have always comforted myself in the knowledge that Kevin had agreed to pursue adoption and that I just sweetened the prospect by accidentally enabling us to share a pregnancy, a delivery of our own baby. The doctor had assured us there was no possibility I could carry Kevin's child full term because of our blood type incompatibility, but my delighted husband did not question the change of events. I'm sure he did not consider the possibility of adultery, of his wife deceiving him. For Kevin, silence was trust.

I did not think I could become pregnant, so I took no precautions when I became close to Rick. There it is. I have said his name. The biological father of my deceased son has no idea he has lost a child. He is a family friend and grieves with us, but he does not realize the severance from a child that our bodies created from long hours of lovemaking at Whimsy Towers. He does not know he has sons.

Rick had lost his wife in a terrible car accident, and he was not looking for romance. They grew up together on the Cape and were newly married when she died. To be ripped from someone you love provides caution in moving on. We both wore wedding rings. I began with the motive of being honorable and trustworthy, but my resolve was short-lived.

With the first load of plants that he brought and planted from the local nursery, we spent time talking and sharing thoughts of relationships and goals. Rick was easy to talk to. He wasn't rushed or distracted. He helped out with the family landscape business that his sister ran. For a few years, he had been taking care of the grass cutting at Whimsy Towers, and he continued when I came that reckless summer of 1980.

Rick opened up slowly about his personal life, and I craved the discovery of intimacy and connection. We often had coffee and conversation out under the lawn umbrella or on the screened porch. I was starved for passion and exploration, and this nice, unsuspecting man had little chance of escaping my clutch. I wanted to be close to him, and I didn't care about the rules.

He was a professor at the local community college, a Ph.D. with a love of crossword puzzles. I was a young woman his age, married yet unsettled. When I began to flirt with him, he wasn't sure how to react. He protested with half-hearted determination, but his goodness could not protect him. Making love outside of marriage was new for both of us. Making love in the middle of the lawn, with soft breezes and sunshine on our exposed bodies, was forbidden pleasure that didn't mind who saw it. We wanted each other with an intensity that had no thought of consequences.

Only my dog Gypsy was at Whimsy Towers to share my attention, and she quickly took on Rick as part of her world. He came often to the house, and we continued to talk and laugh and make love wherever and whenever we felt. We rolled on the Oriental carpets, reaching for pleasure, and then resting in warm satisfaction. He spent afternoons and nights. Rick stumbled into my web and could not get out. He continued to try to protest, to seek the moral ground that was slipping away beneath our feet, but neither of us could let go. We both knew that the make-believe world we were creating could not last, but it was sweet. Decisions needed to be made.

For over two weeks, I gave in to temptation and rarely felt guilt. Kevin remained in Virginia, working long hours at the office and concerned about our being separated. We talked on the phone, and I shared with him the news I was learning about my grandmother

Theodosia. As Kevin learned of her escape to Cape Cod from her South Carolina marriage, he became increasingly concerned that history was repeating itself. I was gathering information about my family and resisting revelations about myself. Could I leave a husband who cared for me?

When it was time to return home, to where I had responsibilities with a husband, it was difficult to face the choices in front of me. Rick urged me to stay on, to continue to explore what we shared, but he knew that obligations pulled me south, to the life I had with a man who was waiting for me. Part of me wanted to abandon a marriage that was suffocating the rebel in me, perhaps the Theodosia in me, but I couldn't honestly blame it all on Kevin.

I'm sure he would never have been brought to romantic temptation. He had internal strength that kept him on course. I doubt Kevin could ever cheat. His lawyerly instincts were to find ways to compromise. He was cautious; I was impulsive. When he ventured into delicate situations with me, especially into confrontation, he tried hard to listen and understand—but with cool detachment. Sometimes we were fire and ice.

I left Whimsy Towers that first time with a heart anxious for change and yet comforted by the familiarity that waited in Virginia. I was eager to share with Kevin all that I had learned about Theodosia and Stormy. I wanted to tell him more about the house with its towers, about whale watching, lobster ravioli, and the beauty of Cape Cod. I wanted to include him, but I savored the memory of Rick and what he had aroused in me. Two men, one heart, one body.

Rick and I said a sad goodbye, but it was a parting that felt right. I cannot say I didn't still long for him in the weeks that followed, but I wanted to work on the relationship at hand, to understand better what I needed in my marriage and how to ask for it. Men are not mind readers, and they do not even share the same vocabulary as women for giving and receiving love. I think men need to be needed, and women need to feel validated. We all yearn to be understood, but resentments get in the way of progress, and marriage becomes a stumbling block, instead of a building block, to happiness. Women close up from frustration, and men shut down from rejection.

I had married a good man and was determined to see change. I wanted to negotiate being upset without demeaning my spouse. I wanted to figure out how to balance disagreement with disapproval, with each of us being heard. There is no healing in criticism. Kevin and I were stuck in the abyss of discouragement. By not talking calmly about our problems and fears, we were really just shutting out the partner that we wanted to be close to, in effect punishing each other.

We desired acceptance and to feel important to the other, but we were hiding in work and self-justification. Denying our feelings and needs might avoid conflict but was also keeping us both from feeling loved. Conflict management is not having a relationship. I would spring the trap. Walking on eggshells is not a healthy lifestyle. Fires needed to be lit.

Women know how to pretend. We are masters at denying our needs for what seems to provide harmony. We try hard to please those around us to keep emotional balance—even living through our husbands' or lovers' accomplishments and interests in order not to threaten them with ours. Unfortunately, I could not reconstruct myself in order to accommodate my husband, but I have to admit that I was probably expecting him to do that for me. None of us is cast in a perfect mold, but fixing a marriage is different from trying to fix the participants. Trying to "fix" another is negating the reasons that he or she is upset; it's saying, "I don't value who you are or how you feel." I think failure of a marriage is the ongoing loss of acceptance and appreciation, and I didn't want to contribute to the demise of mine.

I remember my plan of attack began with three questions. I would work on them each day, like homework for the soul and balm for the future:

1. How could I express more gratitude?
2. How could I better value and appreciate the qualities in Kevin that had made me want to marry him?
3. How could I react less and listen more?

The funny thing is, I didn't expect anything from Kevin. I made no demands and tried to be more alert to temptations that might pull us down a rabbit hole.

Change would have to begin through my own efforts. I practiced withholding judgment. The only thing I could really change was my own thinking and behavior. Assigning blame and feeling resentment were fruitless, just fodder for arguments; and hurtful arguments were not constructive conversation.

My fear was that Kevin would think another woman had moved into my skin, a more patient one—the sure sign of a woman with something to hide. I was not about to relinquish what I liked about myself, but I wanted to stop keeping score and start harvesting happiness. I looked up "empathy" in the dictionary.

Success and setback are the warp and weft of a marriage, but the shuttle determines the pattern and needs a guiding hand. Relationships are not accidental; they are built on caring, and caring is an accumulation of thoughts and deeds.

Kevin reacted well to my change in attitude. As he felt more respected and important, he became more supportive of me. He listened. Love was not dead, just dormant. I was honestly trying to avoid manipulation, but I wanted to steer a new course. You might wonder why I did not suggest marriage counseling. The answer is fear of revelation, fear of being led into unexplored territory that would corner me and reveal transgression. Sometimes I bit my tongue in order to stay silent and protect myself.

It is not Kevin's nature to hold a grudge. He will withdraw and lie low, but he does not pout. Whoever came up with the term "man cave"? A man's safe haven keeps him off the battlefield, but when Kevin could not understand me or my needs, I was no longer willing for him to withdraw.

It is important to say that I was not dealing with an abusive relationship, but one starved for communication, for intimate connection. I was not a victim. Kevin, too, wanted our marriage to survive, to prosper, but we lacked the knowledge and perhaps the energy to revitalize it. We had fallen into routines that did not challenge us. Sometimes I tried to catch him off guard, outside the patterns of his own expectations. I even enticed my unsuspecting husband into making love on the bathroom floor. At first reluctant, his body responded eagerly, and the cool, hard tile added intensity to the heat and abandon of the moment.

How long ago, now, this all seems! We were so young and unaware of what the world would have in store for us. I was certain I could salvage a marriage that had lost its way by the simple force of my determination. I did not realize that deception would be the decisive factor.

Two months later, I knew that I was pregnant. While we were both elated, I doubted that the medical verdict really could have changed. I waited five months before daring to see a doctor, and then I chose a different one who did not know either Kevin or me. There is safety in fresh beginnings, and the doctor saw no problems with the pregnancy or the blood that flowed through the growing baby that I carried. He had no reason to question, and I did not mention miscarriage. We were on our way to having a family, and life was good.

It is easier to reorganize priorities when temptation is not at hand. Rick continued to take care of Whimsy Towers, and we maintained a professional and distant relationship through the year. I mentioned him to Kevin as part of our ongoing ownership of the house, but no alarm bells went off. Kevin does not tend toward suspicion, and gradually the intense feelings I had for Rick softened into certifying my path to reawakened womanhood.

In Virginia, our days were filled with being parents. We named the baby Tim, after my father. It was a generous gesture on Kevin's part. He had been fond of my father and knew his importance in my life as the only parent I knew. My father did not live to see his grandchildren, and our first baby arrived with no grandparents at all to dote on him or to puzzle over family resemblance.

Timmy was born with bright blue eyes, and I remember looking into them, eager for some recognition of his father's; but Rick, too, had piercing blue eyes. Kevin had curly hair, and none of the boys has curly hair. They are all three tall, athletic, and anonymous in their common agility, quick wit, and ready smiles. No peculiar physical function or attribute has betrayed their origin. Rick didn't have bad teeth, big ears, or funny feet; and luckily, neither did Kevin. The boys are smart and thoughtful. I see different characteristics of Rick in them that sometimes cause me to catch my breath and await exposure, but then I remember that I'm the only one alert to the possibilities. Nature and nurture have combined to make handsome young men of promise and likeability.

David was the closest duplicate of the man who is now in his seventies. He looked to me like Rick of long ago. David would surely have grown into an obvious replica of our Cape Cod friend the boys had always known growing up. It is manhood that sets physical identity, and the vagaries of adolescence are just preparation. If David had lived, would observations finally have brought questions? Could a secret survive such obvious contradiction? Would I lie, or let truth wash over all the parties who have been deceived?

I assumed I would have just the one gift of parenthood, one baby conceived from lovemaking off-guard and ill-timed. I came to understand Theodosia's Parisian infidelity and the triumph of her body over the limitations of a boring marriage. There is freedom in letting passion rule. Denying restraint is to thwart convention. Both Theodosia and I reshaped our identities and reclaimed ourselves; but with the addition of a child, I needed to figure out how to earn my marriage.

Unfortunately, complications arise when freedom is bewitched or a suppressed desire reignites. The next summer, I returned again to Whimsy Towers, with a blue-eyed baby just three months old. I had not seen Rick in a year. Kevin remained in Virginia to work on a case.

Chapter Seven

Trust is a fragile thing. It shifts in seasons like the weather. Trust lingers in the imperfections of our hope when we are vulnerable and floats away entirely when we feel unfulfilled in our winters of doubt. Trust is a cycle, and I have often clung to its edges, uncertain of the reliability of renewal. Trust is the temperature of a relationship, the projected feeling of hot and cold in love. Do we attain it or lose it?

"Try this!" boomed my excited son, as he entered the porch with plates of lobster and avocado. The waning afternoon was still bright and breezy, with no hint that the summer sun was moving to its rest behind us. Kev passed out the appetizer of lobster, sliced avocado, and mango. The vinaigrette had a sweet tangy taste on the tongue and perfectly accented the flavors. For me, it would be meal enough, but Kev was just teasing our appetites. More food would follow, and I would happily get myself to the table to enjoy it.

He had chosen old family plates with a floral pattern and gold rim, ancestral relics brought out from the dusty cupboard of another era. I am often reminded of the history at Whimsy Towers, of the interests and loves of those who came before. I have left the many paintings on the walls from Theodosia, Stormy, and their friends.

They painted everywhere, even right onto the wall and the window trim. Some rooms are a riot of color. I have added a few paintings of my own and a few efforts from the boys when they were younger and still under my guidance. Creativity has come in many shapes.

Kev has artistic flair in his food preparation and David the symmetry and harmony of flower arrangement and decoration, but each tucks in a hint of the irregular, a suggestion of disharmony. The predictable in life does not catch the eye.

Our family is firmly rooted in Virginia soil—in Alexandria, where my father brought me, and where Kevin and I also settled—but the boys have wandered with choices that sent them in different directions. Tim was still a teenager when he left for South Carolina and became a husband in anticipation of becoming a father. Spending summers in Cape Cod captured Kevin Jr. and drew him to the Cape in Provincetown after college. David remained close to us, living in Washington, D.C., after graduating from Georgetown University. While David and his laundry could return home to Virginia in twenty minutes, he lived the separate life of a single man in a city invigorated by politics, causes, and an active dating scene. David worked "on the Hill," the euphemism for Congress, Capitol Hill. A Congressional office is a revolving door of smart young talent who have launched from college into helping run busy offices for overwrought politicians.

And that's where this story gets tangled.

I did not know. I just could not have known.

℘

Each summer I returned to Whimsy Towers. I always felt as though part of me was returning home. In 1981 I had owned the house for only one year and had not seen it since my initial visit of just a few weeks. Baby Tim slept and ate and lay on his back, watching clouds move in changing patterns as they drifted out over the ocean. He kicked the air without protest, arms waving, unaware that he would learn to roll over and crawl and then find his own way on two feet. He was easy to have with me while I sketched and wrote, usually outside under the umbrella.

Cape Cod days have a way of laying bare the stress and pretense of life. There is freshness in ocean breezes. I looked out on the lawn and remembered making love with Rick, rolling in the grass, feeling him anxious against my body as we held each other. It was wrong. It was wrong then and would be wrong again, and we had parted with the hope of leaving behind a yearning that had no future.

Rick and I approached each other cautiously that second summer. The first time I saw him, I recognized his old Dodge truck lumbering down the long drive and watched my dog Gypsy rush beyond her usual speed to greet him. Gypsy did not forget a friend. He stepped out and petted her, looking around to assess the scene.

Feelings I thought had diminished surged forth, and for an instant, I was back in the previous June, eager to

see him and to feel his body next to mine. I looked at my
infant son and took a deep breath.

Initial awkwardness gave way to sharing and catching
up on the year's news. Rick knew of my inability to become pregnant with Kevin, and he was surprised and
happy that we had been able to have a child. He did not
question. Part of me wanted to yell, "This is your son!
Let's run away and be together." But I had chosen secrecy and was trying hard to salvage a marriage.

The next day Rick returned to work in the yard. Surrounded by the fresh, earthy fragrance of cut grass, we
discussed plans for some gardens and drank cold tea in
the hot sun. Timmy slept in his basket. I was wearing a
wrap skirt and tank top. I remember there were colorful
fish on the skirt, impossible swimmers set in cotton. We
staked out boundaries for a rose garden and then stood
squinting in the bright light. We both were sweaty and
glistening. Rick was asking about types of roses when I
looked up at him and kissed his cheek. Startled, he
stepped back. I will never forget what he said next: "I
thought we resolved this."

"I thought so, too," I replied, "but I'm not feeling quite
able."

"Theresa, what do you want?"

"I want you close."

Rick said nothing further but enveloped me in his
arms, unwrapping my skirt, and we were soon lying in a
tousle of discarded clothes on freshly cut grass that left
little green bits stuck on moist skin. We made love in the

heat of the afternoon and then went inside and made love again. And again.

Rick stayed, helping me feed and bathe Timmy, and then sharing my grandmother's bed as we listened to night sounds of owls and rustling tree branches, shutting out thoughts of danger, with desire.

We settled into an easy and familiar routine, with Rick staying over most nights. He made coffee while I got the baby ready for the day. We were like a family with a routine. He went off to work, and I continued to write and draw and think only half-heartedly about meals. I often laugh that I have a son whose life revolves around food and meal planning, but Rick is the one who liked to cook.

Kevin checked in almost every day, and we talked about the baby, Whimsy Towers, and his plan of spending more time that summer with us at the Cape. I loved my husband and wanted him to feel loved. I wanted our future to be together. We were now a family, but something in me had room for Rick.

My hope was that Kevin would not surprise me with a visit. I was going to stay at Whimsy Towers all summer, with Kevin flying in once a month. Rick and I accommodated these visits well, and sometimes he joined us for supper or a drink on the lawn with friends I was making in Chatham. We were models of good behavior, but I suppose all guilty lovers feel immune to exposure.

I was totally happy. I was glad to see my husband and enjoyed our days of exploring the area. We took Timmy on outings and tested restaurants all over the Cape.

Kevin had a wife and child, a life complete, a life that didn't beg disruption. Nothing of Rick's stayed in the house to betray another lover's presence. Kevin and I easily filled the hours together, loving each other and our wonderful baby fathered by an unknowing guest. Rick was not thrilled with this arrangement, but he accepted the reality of wanting our time together more than a willingness to give it up.

Was it foolishness or hopefulness that kept me from using birth control with Rick? Either way, I did not. The first summer was ignorance and the impossibility I assumed, but I had not made a plan to be intimate with him again. The realization that I could become pregnant with a man not my husband, with medical barriers removed, opened the possibility of more children. I wanted Rick sexually and did not at first stop to consider the ramifications, but then I abandoned thoughts of protection and safety from pregnancy. If making love with this man resulted in more children, I would welcome the idea of growing my family with Kevin. I was cheating two men.

We were all satisfied, for the moment.

In the next three years, I gave birth to two more springtime babies. I arrived in June, eager for Rick, and then returned to Whimsy Towers with the results of our imprudence. I balanced my feelings with the greedy longing to have my own way. I was aroused, challenged, intrigued, and satisfied by the men I loved.

How many years we would have continued the devil-may-care paradigm I cannot say. A second child created complications for intimacy. A toddler does not sit still.

Rick and I modified our behavior, trying to avoid too many questions from Timmy or being naked in his presence. Rick spent less time at Whimsy Towers. I missed our long conversations, laughter, and crossword puzzle challenges. Rick was funny, optimistic. We connected easily. He was an intelligent and handsome package, like Kevin, but more accessible to my moods. I could light a fire under Kevin for physical connection, but Rick brought his own fire.

The summer that I arrived with two little boys and new baby David, Rick met me at the house with a sheepish grin. He lifted and hugged the boys, kissed me only gently, and tried to gather his thoughts. He had met someone. A new professor at the college had arrived from Germany, and they had gotten serious over the academic year. He wanted to give the relationship a chance, and he could not deceive her with another woman.

Honesty is a grand endeavor. I am obviously not very good at it, but Rick was a master of self-control, and I felt the hidden anguish of moral clarity. He had to choose, and he was betting on his own life.

The simple story is that he married a young, talented, bilingual woman who took my place and usurped my role as lover and confidante. The next summer they were expecting a baby, and Rick was finding his fatherhood.

Their daughter Susan was born in Chatham and became a welcome playmate to three older boys who saw her regularly in the summers. She and David were

closest in age and became best friends at swimming lessons and exploring the nooks and crannies of the shoreline. They captured and released frogs, played Twister in
the boathouse, and roasted marshmallows in the fire pit
that Rick built in the garden. They even took sailing lessons together, which unsteadied my nerves.

Our families were comfortable together, and our ad-
justed situation met the needs of both the children and
adults. Whimsy Towers was a hub for friendship, and
children came and went. Rick continued to take care of
Whimsy Towers until his daughter, an only child, consumed more of his time and their family interests took
precedence over maintenance of my house. We had no
unguarded moments, and gradually our past indiscretions dissolved into the history of emotional upheaval in
bygone youth.

David and Susan were inseparable as youngsters, but
toward the end of high school and throughout college,
David spent his summers working in D.C. He rarely
came to the Cape, except for occasional Thanksgivings
that we shared with neighbors and friends. He was an
intern for our Congressman, and after college, they offered him a full-time job.

Everything ignited, however, when one day he ran
into Susan at the Congressional cafeteria in the Rayburn
Building on Independence Avenue. Unknown to Kevin
and me, David began dating his childhood friend, seeing
her regularly after work and beginning to take weekend
outings together. She had landed a good job with a New
England congressman and was living in D.C. with

roommates. David had no other eyes or ears in his apartment, and she spent increasing amounts of time with him. When he finally shared this information with Kevin and me, I was dumbstruck. My unsuspecting son was falling in love with his own half sister.

Chapter Eight

I was comfortable on the lounge, with a cashmere coverlet that I don't remember putting over myself. The men in my life are attentive to me when they are around, perhaps because they see increasing opportunities to be of help. I'm alarmed when I can't pull together thoughts or remember what someone has just told me. It's distressing to realize that the mental capacities that have brought me success in my work, and especially my writing, are the very instrument for present failures.

Brad began the conversation about Kev's lobster appetizer. "These flavors are amazing. What's in this mayonnaise?"

"Luckily, I know that Whimsy Towers has a great herb garden, and I can always find whatever I need. The secret is tarragon. It adds a unique flavor and subtle texture and is perfect with the lobster."

I nodded agreement and took a bite of the mango with sweet pepper vinaigrette. Without warning, tears began to form and started to slide down my cheeks. I looked down to regain composure, but short gasps of breath gave me away.

"Mother, what is it? What's the matter?"

I swallowed and tried to smile at my son. "Mango was David's favorite. He's the one who taught me how to cut one open, and we used to share the drippy mess of getting every last bite from around the pit." I paused. "I'm glad my best memories of David are laughter."

"I'm so sorry, Mom."

"No, it's fine. In a way, we are celebrating him. Mango was his guilty pleasure. David was so focused in his work on reducing carbon in the atmosphere, dealing with industry and communities to minimize their carbon emissions. Personally, he tried to buy products and produce that weren't shipped thousands of miles from their source. He felt there was no justification for buying a mango in winter that had to be flown in from the Philippines, but David just loved them and couldn't help it. He was a 'buy local' guy, and he helped me be a better consumer. The environment was his number one issue. I will miss his prodding about consumer choices."

"He called us all!" Kev laughed. "He was very determined to improve eating habits, but I have often wondered at how we have such abundance and variety in our food, and yet obesity rates keep skyrocketing. Choice should foster more thoughtful selection."

"I love your optimism, Kev," I answered, "but pizza, hamburgers, and French fries are American cuisine. Vegetables are enemy invaders."

"I do think Americans are more interested in ethnic food these days. Perhaps because of more travel abroad or perhaps because we have so many immigrants from countries that are bringing their tastes and culture."

"Thank God for that," added Brad. "Diversity is fuel."

"What an odd and wonderful concept," said Kev. "We are moved forward by what pushes us."

Brad looked at me and then turned to Kev. "There is something I want to talk to you about. Perhaps this is as good a time as any, before the next few days get too busy and complicated." He stopped to gather his thoughts. "Kev, I love our life together. I never dreamed I would find a partner so loving and supportive. And fun. I believe we fit. And I believe we are complete. That said, you know I have hoped someday we might have children, or a child, and we've talked about it. You grew up in a happy home, with two brothers and parents who cared for you unconditionally. You know I did not. I ache for that sense of family and belonging." Brad stopped, and Kev reached out to hold his hand, waiting.

"I know someone in Boston who is in a position to place an infant boy. His mother does not want him, cannot take care of him, and the state will determine where he goes. I'd like him to be ours. Would you consider it?"

Kev did something I had never before witnessed. He moved closer to Brad and tenderly wrapped his arms around the man he loved. I think they shared a moment of revelation, a turning point in commitment, and then Kev replied simply, "Of course."

"Really? It's a big step."

"It's important to you, and you are important to me. I think we have room in our hearts for a little guy who will grow up to make us crazy!" Kev looked toward me and laughed.

LOVE & LIES | 73

"There's more," continued Brad, slowly. "He has drugs in his system and is slowly going through withdrawal. His mother is an opioid addict. And he's biracial. Would you like to see him?" Without waiting for an answer, Brad took out his phone and brought up a photo the agency had sent him.

A tiny black baby wearing an orange knit cap was lying on a plaid blanket. Brad touched the screen, and the baby began to kick and cry, with a wrenching sound that left no doubt of his distress. An easy road did not lie ahead.

"Can we deal with this?" asked Brad. "Can we love a child that was someone's mistake? He would be our son, not a project or a pet. He would change us forever. I know that this timing is unfortunate, and I'm so sorry to add complication to such a sad time. I would understand if you want to wait."

"I'm willing to be all in," said Kev, holding Brad's hand. "We will be partners in love, in life, and in parenting. Others before us have taken on this challenge, and we can, too. I say, Yes."

They kissed briefly, and I was the observer of a remarkable moment. I was an absent mother and a present witness, observing how what we have chosen and what we desire can come together. Brad and Kev were moving from one phase of life to another, and they shared an expectation of good things to come.

Relationships and marriages are not automatically a solution to individual hopes. Relationships must be made happy, made to conform to collective intent. I was watching two men who defied convention by loving each other and now wanted to broaden that base of caring to include a child not of their own making. Purposeful connections create the basis of home, and I hoped that both men would find that sense of yearning satisfied.

They were not afraid to make choices for which there is no guarantee. Brad and Kev give me hope for the future. They are fearless, generous, and devoted. Hope resides in the possibility of a better future; and while we are not in charge of the future, our present behavior molds it in small ways that build bonds. They will be good parents, and a lost little boy will find home.

Kev and Brad immediately turned to their phones and began the process of contacting the agency and making plans to go to Boston to see the baby. They were beginning a journey of no return, a validation of newness. I think the purpose of life is to be alert to possibilities, sometimes to take the road less traveled because we dare.

I sat quietly a moment and thought of David, of his enthusiasm and kindness. I didn't want to return to the rituals of grief when the squeals of new life bespoke the future. My thoughts wandered to family that would be arriving the next day for our farewell to David. Kevin will connect with Tim and his friend, as yet nameless, at the airport in Boston and drive together to the Cape. Kevin will be too polite to drill his oldest son, but he is aware that Tim's wife has a weekend replacement. I doubt Tim is expecting two bedrooms.

As if reading my mind, Mattie came onto the porch to clear the dishes and asked, "How many bedrooms do you want made up?"

"I think we are trying to be flexible. Kev and Brad will stay, so let's just be at full strength operation to accommodate tomorrow's arrivals. We'll see what happens." With Mattie in one bedroom, there are still four bedrooms for family use, all with private baths and wonderful views. Fragrance and ocean breezes find their way. There are no neglected or uninviting rooms at Whimsy Towers. Each has a personality and beckons.

"Well, that's it," announced Kev. "We're going to Boston next week for an interview and to see how parenthood might feel. I admit I'm rather excited."

"You are incredible," replied Brad. "Half an hour ago, your world was pretty much fixed and safe, and now you're willing to leap into the abyss."

Kev smiled. "But I'm leaping with you." Then he got up and turned to us as he left the porch, "How about some dinner?"

Brad and I looked at each other and laughed. "Was that easier than you thought?" I asked.

"Much easier. But I cannot help but think in some way that David's death softened him for this."

"And perhaps seeing his own parents aging? There is a cycle of giving and taking care. It seems one minute we are taking care of babies and then the next needing taking care ourselves. You know his father and I will help you any way we can, for as long as we can. I think it's just wonderful, and I may soon be a grandmother!"

Brad gave me a long hug, with tears in his eyes. "There are still lots of details to work out, financial verifications, background checks, and the obvious need to accommodate a baby in our house."

"You will be fine," I assured him. "Luckily, you have time to grow into being parents; the logistics will fall into place. Tim was actually born at home and spent his first night in his father's underwear drawer!" Brad looked startled. "Babies allow us to build our fortresses slowly. And don't underestimate a jealous cat! Your feline addition may not welcome another. I have a photograph of Kev sleeping in his crib with our tabby cat close to him. The cat approached him only when there was peaceful silence. At first stir, Sully slipped away; but a purring sound must have been soothing from a warm, soft animal that liked to snuggle in the night."

Brad went to join Kev in the kitchen, and I could hear them talking excitedly. Pans rattled, cupboards closed, silverware clinked. They were operating in a space they understood and shared, but what must be going through their heads: disbelief, anticipation, fear? Their daily habits will change. I give gratitude every morning before my feet hit the floor for the three children in my life. We learn about ourselves through others, and my children have been the means for past versions of myself to adapt and grow. Self-discovery is ongoing.

While society lives in a continual war for material accumulation, my sons have seen their father's reflective desire for aspirations in a moral context. They are young men with heart, with awareness of community needs.

They volunteer, they give; but severing the umbilical cord cast them into a world leading away from their mother. Do all mothers with grown offspring long for their dependent, adoring, little ones? Do I yearn for my youth by wishing my children had not left theirs?

The sobering fact is that my sons no longer have need of me. They do not question; they do not pry. They are not unkind, but I am an attachment at arms' length.

My boys are just living their own lives, and I suppose they assume I am doing the same. But I am increasingly slipping from those I love. I feel it creeping up on me. My sons are mostly absent from my life now, and I don't want them to be absent from my mind. Genes are not destiny, but I am struggling not to follow Theodosia. Memory is a gift not to be taken for granted. It holds all my yesterdays.

I think it's easier to stay in the past, because I know my way there.

Chapter Nine

Mattie had made omelets with lobster and bell peppers. A white cheese oozed out the edges. Corn muffins were fresh from the oven, filling the house with the aroma of her southern contribution to a New England breakfast. She brought coffee to my bedroom in the morning, letting Kev and Brad sleep in. Our dinner had been a celebration of adoption, but I retired early, letting the two men stay up late with their questions and dreams. A new day brought the challenges of accommodating both death and new life.

Bright sunshine filled the porch and reached over the table, warming the back of my head and shoulders. Mornings in Cape Cod are about light, the gift of a huge ball of glowing wonder that rises from the watery horizon, sprinkled with orange and yellow that disappears in wandering ripples. The ocean sings, soothes, and keeps me company. I am content here, happy as an arsonist on a hayride.

"What shall we have for lunch today when everyone arrives?" Mattie asked as she refilled my coffee cup.

"Clam chowder and corn muffins would be great. Did you make enough?"

"Oh yes, I'm stocked up with the staples. Do you know when they'll get here?"

"I think we'll be having a late lunch," I replied, feeling both eager and apprehensive about seeing Kevin for the first time since David's death. I've been trying to grasp the sequence of events from the accident and have mostly gaps in remembering. Kevin will want answers; he will want to know details of how his youngest son could die in front of a subway train in New York City. I am both anxious and afraid to understand. My mind is fighting me.

"Good morning!" boomed Kev, as he and Brad entered the porch with cups already filled with coffee. They both stooped to kiss me and sat down with the familiarity and ease of doing it every day. I had the sudden thought that Whimsy Towers would one day be theirs, theirs and their son's, and this porch would entertain and charm their family and friends for many years after I am gone. Who will be the guardian of Theodosia's treasure?

Mattie had added fresh flowers to the drooping arrangement that David left on the porch table. New blossoms invigorated the old. She brought breakfast to the two chefs, who thanked and appreciated her. "What beautiful plating," remarked Brad, rotating his breakfast to show its most aesthetically pleasing angle. Sliced grapes, pineapple, cantaloupe, and pomegranate seeds hugged the omelet at the edge of the plate, with a sprig of mint and small dollop of flavored honey.

"People in the restaurant are always taking pictures of their food," added Kev. "It's a funny habit, but it's great advertising for us. We've even had people come in and show us a picture on their phone to order what they want to eat."

We moved slowly through breakfast, enjoying the calm, the sun, the pleasure of company that would forever be altered by adding a child.

"Is there anything we can do to help you this morning, Theresa? We've got dinner covered, but Kev and I want to be useful."

"Thank you, Brad. Perhaps a last-minute grocery run for Mattie. She usually does it, but she's readying the house and would probably be glad for the help. I'll get a list and would like to go along, to walk a little and to get out of the way of the caterers. They'll be here soon to set up for tomorrow, but Mattie is the event planner. She can juggle the moving parts better than I."

I want to accommodate the life changes that are coming. I want to adjust. I need to adjust. I'm trying not to hold on to yesterday, but I know the future will have no resemblance to the past or even to the present. A biblical passage from Ecclesiastes became the basis of a folk song that was almost an anthem for my youth in the 1960s, a plea of causes and rebellion and change:

> To everything there is a season,
> and a time to every purpose under the heaven:
> A time to be born, and a time to die;
> a time to plant,
> and a time to pluck up that which is planted;
> A time to kill, and a time to heal;
> a time to break down, and a time to build up;

A time to weep, and a time to laugh;
 a time to mourn, and a time to dance;
A time to cast away stones,
 and a time to gather stones together;
A time to embrace,
 and a time to refrain from embracing;
A time to get, and a time to lose;
 a time to keep, and a time to cast away;
A time to rend, and a time to sew;
 a time to keep silence, and a time to speak;
A time to love, and a time to hate;
 a time of war, and a time of peace.

What is the cue that society is ready for a shift? How will I make the personal shift to life without David?

In 2005 I went to the U.S. Capitol in Washington to view the casket of Rosa Parks lying in repose. I waited in a long, curving line for six hours for the opportunity to pay respect to a civil rights pioneer who took a stand in 1955. Keeping her seat on an Alabama bus was her statement of determination. There were few white faces in that solemn line. I didn't get into the Rotunda until well after midnight, long past the time that security expected to allow viewing.

When to wait and when to pounce are the strategies of life. Social structure is not fixed for all time. I have lived to see a black man as president of the United States. A smart, articulate, funny, and able man who happened to be black dared to stand up for his abilities—unthinkable just a few decades ago.

When David was a teenager, he and I visited Robben Island, near Cape Town, South Africa, and saw the tiny cell where Nelson Mandela spent eighteen of the twenty-seven years he was in prison. Breaking rocks all day in the hot courtyard, Mandela groomed his mind for things to come. He dared to see the possibilities of humanity. Mandela, too, became president of his country, overcoming the suppression of the white majority.

Dare to hope, dare to challenge, dare to speak truth to power. Examples of great resolve encourage us lesser mortals to be more alert to daily choices. *"A time to break down, and a time to build up." "A time to keep, and a time to cast away."* Who is the judge of a life well lived?

"If I am a body that functions, but without adequate mental capacity, who am I?" I heard myself say aloud.

Both Kev and Brad stared at me. "What do you mean, Mother? What are you talking about?"

"Oh, I'm so sorry." I sat up straight in my chair. "I was just wandering. I feel a little dizzy, and there's an odd ringing in my ears."

"Do you think you should go out?" Brad asked. "We can shake down the grocery list, while you have a rest."

"No, no, I'll be fine. I'd like an outing before the others come. Let's see what Mattie needs."

Kevin Jr. took our plates to the kitchen and returned with a list in his head of six items for Mattie. I could never trust myself with that. What is not written is lost. Even my organized father used to say, "I have a good memory, but it's short." Kev was trained in food minutiae, and he was comfortable with the responsibility.

We climbed into my son's SUV and headed down the driveway, passing the caterers. I felt we were in a lumbering tank on a land reconnaissance mission. Bumps in the road seemed more pronounced from the higher vantage point. For me, climbing into the tank was comfortable; getting out required a steady helper.

We parked easily and walked arm in arm into the store. I pushed the cart to give me balance and headed down the produce aisle as Brad and Kev scouted the items for Mattie. Turning a corner, I nearly collided with Rick and his daughter Susan.

"So sorry, wild driver!" I exclaimed, as I veered to the side.

"Theresa, how are you? We were just talking about you. Is there anything we can do to help with the funeral or at the house?" Rick asked, his eyes meeting mine without hesitation. Those blue eyes were also David's, and they were lost to me again. "We'll see you tomorrow, but we're so sad for this occasion and wish we could lighten your load. We still can't believe it. To lose your child is unimaginable."

Susan reached into her pocket for a tissue, dabbing her eyes.

I automatically stepped over to hug her. I could easily hug and cherish her now, knowing she would not be part of David's life. In death we could share him. She had loved my son; that was enough for the record. The need to separate David from her was a futile battle that I might not have won without truth telling that would ruin more than their relationship. He could not marry his sister,

even a half sister, but there was no reasonable reason except the one that could not be spoken. She is a delightful
and caring young woman. Her puffy face betrayed her
sorrow, and I wanted to comfort her.

"Thanks, Rick, but there is nothing. All the troops will
be in today. We'll see you tomorrow; and remember, we
want you to come back for dinner. It will be just our family and yours." We said goodbye and hugged the way
older people hug—awkwardly, without a connection
that stirs emotion—in front of a pile of overripe man-
goes. The sweet scent of remembering made my fragile
heart ache.

I turned the cart around and aimed toward the back
of the store. I had no shopping assignment and was looking for Brad and Kev. My head hurt, and the ringing per-
sisted. I turned several corners, hoping for familiar faces
but finding long aisles of new territory. I doubled back
on my path, mixing up the aisles. I was lost. The tall
shelves towered over me and seemed too close. I needed
to find a way out. Tightening my grip, I pushed a little
faster and nearly tipped over the empty cart. I sped past
cereal and cookies, soup and spices. "Kev, where are
you?" I felt hot and faint. I needed air.

Then a large display of tomato juice in glass bottles
appeared to jump in front of me, and I ran straight into
it, shattering glass and sending juice everywhere. I
slipped on the sticky puddles and fell into the mess,
bringing the cart on top of me. The sound of glass breaking repeated in my head in slow motion.

The crash brought several shoppers to my aid, carefully navigating the dangerous remnants of glass bottles and the slippery floor. They gazed wide-eyed. Clearly, no one wanted to touch the lady bleeding from broken glass, clothes and hair soaked in red slime. "Assistance on aisle seven" filled the air. "Customer needs assistance, please. Code one." The circle of disbelievers widened, and soon I saw my startled son. A store employee came up behind him.

"Mother, what happened? Are you all right? Can you hear me?"

The next thing I remember is the ambulance ride.

I could not stay present. Consciousness seemed a state of visitation. My mind denied my body, fighting to be free of it. I could not satisfy the demand of my body to be in control and in pain and also to honor the mental need to subdue it. I had to take charge, not to accept the power of an accident. I was not ready to relinquish myself.

"I will fight," a voice said aloud, speaking softly from a hidden inventory of hope. "I can fight. I must fight."

"Of course you can, Mother. Stay with us. I'm here. It's Kev. Can you hear me? Please, Mother, don't go. Stay with me." I was aware of someone holding my hand, and I could not pull back or move on.

I awoke fully to find myself in a bed of crisp, white sheets. I was covered in bandages. Every part of me hurt, and my head felt as though a hundred hands were pushing against it, trying to make a shape from clay. One eye did not work.

"Thank God!" a familiar voice said. Kevin was at my bedside. "You've scared us, Theresa," continued my husband, his face red with anxiety and fear. "We came straight from the airport."

"We?" I asked, not yet grasping the situation.

"Yes, I called Mattie when we landed, and she told me what happened. Kev had called her. Theresa, I've been so frightened. I'm so sorry I was not here. I should have come last night." Tears fell onto the sheet tucked tightly around me.

I was still on the "we." "Who's 'we'?"

"Tim and Melanie. The hospital would only allow family in, so Tim's driven her to the house in the rental car. Brad is downstairs with Kev and would not leave."

"Who's Melanie?"

"My darling Theresa, you've had a shock, a bad concussion and a fall. Let's take this slowly. Melanie is Tim's guest for the weekend."

I closed what may have been only one eye. "'Melanie,' a Halloween costume for Elizabeth. What's she like?"

"Well, she's nice. She has bright red hair and seems to like Tim quite a bit. I get the feeling this is not their first trip together. But let's focus on you. How do you feel?"

"I feel as though I want to get up and go home. I can't wait around here. Tomorrow is David's funeral. I need to be there."

Kevin hesitated. "They are talking about keeping you overnight. You had a lot of glass stuck in you and lost a lot of blood. Miraculously, nothing is broken."

"No, Kevin, please, I need to get out." I tried to lift my body but could not make it obey.

"Theresa, you're not moving until the doctors give the 'all clear.' We'll deal with tomorrow when we have to."

Kevin brought a steadiness to my life, the tail on my kite. He was not easily unsettled, but I could see that I had scared him. I had no idea what I looked like, but my arms were wrapped, and I could feel that something covered part of my face.

"Kevin, do I look like a living mummy?"

He laughed. "I like the 'living' part. You are tough, Theresa, and we'll face this together. You will be all right. We will be all right. Please rest, and I'll be back shortly. Now that you're awake, I want to find out what the prognosis is."

As Kevin left, Kev stuck his head in the door and said briefly, "Hi Mom, you would have been a YouTube sensation, if the crash had been filmed. Pretty dramatic stuff. You really frightened us, and I'm so glad you're doing all right. Brad sends love."

I wanted to roll on my side but could not. I no longer had the mental control pad for movement. I felt lost, helpless, and vulnerable.

Sleep found me.

 emsp; ❦

The room had darkened when I woke up. Low lights provided enough illumination to see furniture, the door to the bathroom, some flowers on the table, and three handsome faces in silent vigil. My husband and sons were waiting for me. Not a cell phone to be seen or heard, not a whisper of conversation. They just waited.

"What's happened? What day is this?"

Kevin answered, "They're going to keep you overnight for observation, Theresa. The blood loss is a concern and has made you weak and disoriented. The wounds need to be monitored and cleaned. And you have considerable bruising."

"Disoriented? I think we can all assume that that's what led to this embarrassment, not the result of it. I should have been more careful."

"Never mind all that, Mother. You are going to be fine. The grocery store has called to check on you and send good wishes. I suppose they wonder if our people will be in touch with their people!"

"Oh, Kev, it was my own foolishness, not their fault. We must pay for the breakage. And when can I get out?"

"Well," Kevin began, "they will release you in the morning for the day, if you agree to stay in a wheelchair and return tomorrow evening. They are not saying if you will need to be readmitted. I guess it depends how the day goes. Will you cooperate?"

"Do I have a choice?"

"No, and there will be many eyes on you to assure compliance. You should be able to get to the bathroom with help, but otherwise, you are chair-bound. You would likely lose your balance if you try walking too soon."

"How are the preparations at home?"

"Mattie has everything under control with the caterers. The marquee is up in the yard, the tables for food and drinks are ready, and there are plenty of chairs. The flowers are fabulous, and more will arrive tomorrow. David would like that."

"Oh, Kevin, I should be there."

"They will deliver the urn when you are home, so you can receive David's ashes." He paused. "Theresa, we have so much to talk about, but you must take it easy."

"I understand, and I will try."

The outline of my body under the bed covers was an exaggeration of my shape. I couldn't move my legs and assumed they were enlarged from bandaging. I didn't want to be in a hospital gown for David's funeral. A mother should look prepared, and I would need help. The service was not until 11:00, so there was time to get myself ready. The funeral parlor had agreed to bring the music and organization to Whimsy Towers, so at least I wouldn't need to be travelling. We'd celebrate David where other family members have departed.

"Okay then, we have a plan," my lawyer husband announced. "We are going home now to Kev's delicious scallops and will return in the morning to get you and the wheelchair in his SUV. Your dinner is on its way—all liquid, I'm afraid."

"Thank you for staying," I managed to say as the three tall men each bent to kiss my bandaged face.

I had made a muddle of the day and could not hide from it. Tomorrow I would say goodbye to my child, meet a woman who is positioning herself in my son's marriage, and need to explain why a simple excursion to the grocery store had ended in a wheelchair.

Chapter Ten

Folding chairs lined up in tidy rows faced the ocean. Sailboats of varying sizes glided past, close to shore, but far enough out to catch the summer breezes that challenged both tourists and locals. The sails were like handkerchiefs braced in the wind, holding their steady angles to maintain course with grace and speed.

Sailing has always eluded me. It represents disruption of order, relinquishing the familiar for a wet wilderness that has different rules. Truth is, I am afraid. Poseidon holds the skilled and the weary in his grasp, ready to call them into his submerged realm. There is no certainty on land, but I think a person is always a foreigner at sea, a visitor to circumstances that relentlessly test our talents. I cannot master two worlds. My mother tried—and lost.

Whimsy Towers has been an anchor of happiness and a landscape of grief. Oddly, my son David was the only sailor in our family. He and Susan sailed together as children; and though he remained primarily in Virginia, he loved the opportunity to be at the helm when he came to Chatham. I was reluctant crew, but Kevin has always enthusiastically shared his sons' interests. He knows how to participate and how to give space.

Bedrooms had been assigned while I was in the hospital. With only one for Tim and Melanie, it was decided that I would have the extra one, if I was allowed to stay home. Sleeping alone would be safer for my injuries.

Waiting at the door when we pulled up was a striking Asian woman with bright red hair. She hurried out to help with the wheelchair. "Hello, I'm Melanie."

"How do you do, Melanie. I'm sorry I was not here to greet you yesterday. I'm afraid I created quite a ruckus."

"We're glad you are safely home."

"Thank you," I replied, noting the familiarity. "I hope you're settling in all right."

"Oh yes, it's so beautiful here, and Tim and I had an early walk down the beach this morning. Mattie says she will have a few little jobs for me later."

Mattie was protective of our family; perhaps she was just putting off the flame-haired marriage wrecker.

"Melanie, shall we have a coffee on the porch while the men move chairs around? I'm a little too tired to start getting ready for the funeral. The boys will need to carry me upstairs, but I'd like to wait thirty minutes or so. Will you join me?"

We settled into cushioned chairs facing the ocean. The lawn had been freshly mowed, and the scent of cut grass filled the porch until Mattie arrived with a tray of steaming coffee.

"Tell me about yourself, Melanie."

She hesitated. "You are very kind to allow me to come with Tim. I suppose it's a little shocking."

"My dear, I have grown sons, and they are able to figure out their own lives. I'm fond of Elizabeth, but I know it has not been easy for Tim. You are most welcome here because Tim wants you here. Is this something serious?"

She looked a little startled. "I don't think so. Not for me, anyway. We live in the same small town in South Carolina, but we mostly travel to be together. It's risky. He makes excuses for a business trip or family visit, and we get away together. I've lived there my whole life."

I wondered how many phantom family visits I had missed. We were a good excuse, just not a real destination.

"Do you work there?"

She smiled and replied, "I'm an e-Bay entrepreneur. I resell things online. I'm also working on a Masters degree in Religious Studies through an online program. I spend a lot of my day staring at a computer screen. In my free time I tutor special needs children. I have a twin sister with a disability." She stared out at the huge clouds rolling above the distant horizon like a caravan of tumbling pillows. "I think we find time for what we value."

We sipped our coffee and enjoyed the breeze that found its way across the lawn from the ocean. Clearly, this young woman was more substantial than a weekend convenience.

She continued. "My father was in the last Peace Corps program in South Korea. In 1981 he returned home with fluent Korean and a woman to speak it with. They married, and nine months and four days later, my sister and I were born. My Korean mother was so thrilled to be in the United States, in the south, in what she thought was the land of *Gone with the Wind*. Can you guess what my twin sister's name is?"

I laughed. "Scarlett?"

"Yes, though our two natures are the opposite of the original characters. She is the gentle, kind, and forgiving one!"

"You seem to have a busy life, Melanie." I paused. "Pardon me, but what are you hoping for from this relationship?"

"I do care about Tim. Perhaps it's hard for you to understand, for your generation, but I'm in this relationship for the pleasure of it. I don't mean to embarrass you, but Tim is great to be with. And he's kind and smart; I love his company. He doesn't really know, and doesn't ask, but I see other men, too. Tim is devoted to his wife, which I find rather charming—and challenging. He struggles with being unfaithful, but I like to pull him away from even thinking about her. I want us to be so all-consuming in his mind and body that he can hardly wait to be with me."

"How long have you been seeing each other?"

"About five years. At first we met in the basement of the library; it was dark and private. Then we began to meet in the next town for afternoons. A married man in a small town coming to my house would create too much attention. This trip is wonderful, and we've planned on taking more than a week away."

"And that's enough?"

"Do you mean the time or the relationship?"

"I suppose both."

"Well, the time is enough because we've never been together long enough to get bored or settle into patterns that might be irritating or demanding. The relationship is enough because we each get from it what satisfies us."

"And Tim shares that view?"

"I think so. I suppose so. He really doesn't have a choice, and he would be guilt-ridden no matter what—for cheating in an unhappy marriage or for leaving it. Poor guy has a conscience. He just also has male desires. Please know, Tim was not the one to instigate this."

"Well, Melanie, I appreciate your being so candid with me. I hope neither of you will get hurt."

I completely understood her. I understood the need to have what is physically desirable in the midst of what is predictable and given, but the craving for arousal and risk is not defensible when it crosses your path like a black cat.

"I don't exactly see us growing old together, but I do not have any intention of hurting Tim's wife. Seems she has created her own bubble of happiness, alcoholic happiness. She has turned from him, excluding him, and he has found a way to compensate. For me, I am not deceiving anyone. The men in my life do not expect to be exclusive. I enjoy variety. My father is a farmer. He is careful to rotate his crops, nourishing the soil to get the best harvest each year. The soil can become stagnate and barren if not furnished with fresh nutrients. I am like that soil that needs replenishing."

"Goodness, I think I will leave with that analogy and get myself dressed. I'm glad we've had a chance to chat,

Melanie. Could you please ask Tim and my husband to come help me upstairs?"

I had met my match in the temptress category and realized that my son had no chance of escape. As long as he was content with the arrangement, nothing would disrupt their pleasure. I couldn't help but wonder what would ultimately tip the boat.

Strong arms carried me upstairs, like an Egyptian princess straddled on a throne between her laborers.

"You okay with this weight, Dad?"

"I'm fine," replied Kevin, breathing heavily.

They gently laid me on the bed and then began the process of finding clothes that could fit over bandages that covered most of my body. This day was not going to be about fashion.

Guests began to arrive shortly before 11:00. A blue and white urn held David's ashes and was placed on a low table loaded with flowers in front of the chairs. The blue of the ocean was a striking backdrop to the clusters of bright reds, orange, and yellow blossoms. White roses popped out amidst the color, as if to signal "Surprise!" We had not yet decided what to do with the ashes. Should they be buried, scattered, or taken to sea? Kevin and I had conversations ahead, but for today, David would remain with us and be at the dinner in his honor.

Rick and his family were among the first to arrive. Susan leaned heavily on her father's arm, sobbing openly when she saw the urn. Young love cannot grasp the long road that lies ahead, and she looked like a woman who had folded up her life and sent it away. I had learned from David how much he loved her and that they were making plans for a life together. She must have felt not only desperately lonely, but cheated.

Music of flutes and violins began to waft across the lawn, filling the air with calm and reverence. Guests took their seats and stared ahead, silent in their own musings. We had prepared for thirty, and the seats were almost filled: boyhood friends, neighbors, sailing and drinking buddies, and even his Boy Scout troop leader from Virginia, who happened to be vacationing on the Cape and saw the notice in the paper. Some I knew; many I did not. David would be more remembered as an adult in Virginia and D.C., and we planned to do a memorial service for him there as well, but our family needed remembering at Whimsy Towers.

The mood shifted as more lively piano music began to pound forth. Scott Joplin got our feet tapping to ragtime. His lively and familiar "Entertainer" cannot help but lift spirits, though "Maple Leaf Rag" is one of my favorites. The somber mood was over; Shubert and Bach were not among the remaining guests. People began to strike up conversations, and the solemnity of an expected dirge dissipated. Kevin stepped in front of the group, and the music stopped.

"Friends, thank you for coming today to pay tribute and to say goodbye to our son David. While we lament his tragic loss, we celebrate his wonderful life. He was a blessing to Theresa and me, and we watched with gratitude our last child grow into an outstanding, thoughtful young man.

"Many of you will join me in remembering his boom-ing greeting of 'Jambo,' which is 'Hello' in Swahili, or 'Mambo,' 'What's up?' Each of our boys took a special trip with his mother when they turned sixteen. David and Theresa spent their two-week, mother-son trip in Africa, where he went on safari, visited a Massai village, and fell in love with African culture. If he had not been offered a great job right out of college, I'm sure he would have found his way back to Tanzania or Ghana.

"'Hakuna matata' rolled off David's lips easily in the midst of commotion or uncertainty. It means 'No wor-ries' in Swahili and more than once broke the spell of stress. David had a way of sensing the needs of others. He was politically adept and personally attentive. He was gifted and kind. And he was in love with a childhood friend, Susan, who grieves with us today and who will always be part of our family.

"Our other two boys will both speak this morning, and then we invite you to share memories as well."

Tim stood and shyly faced the crowd from his seat.

"We three were all close in age. Our parents had a slow start at it, and then they just couldn't seem to stop. David was the last, and he was our scapegoat. Kev and I used to set him up for trouble. If something broke, 'Da-vid did it.' If we were late coming in for dinner, 'David held us up.' Too many cookies missing? 'David ate them.' We used the poor little guy like a mop to tidy up our messes. But then he began to grow up, and we totally lost our power over him.

"One story comes to mind that I wasn't sure I would ever share. When I was about eight, and he was four, we were digging around in Mom's stuff and found an old metal box. It was full of papers and, clearly, none of our business. However, at the bottom were some cards that had pictures of baseball players. We didn't really know many famous baseball players, but we liked the cards. And one was of Mickey Mantle, which David thought was cool because it sounded like Mickey Mouse.

"Most of the cards were in color, some with an odd, tinted look, but about half a dozen were old black and white, almost sepia. Well, David decided he would color up the dull-looking cards to make them more pretty for Mom, so we took three of them. I remember their funny team name was Boston Red Stockings. I took two of the colored cards, the Mickey Mantle and a Willie Mays.

"Some of you may be gasping about now, and with reason. The roots of Boston baseball came from the Red Stockings, early pioneers of the Hall of Fame. The 1872 team finished first in the National Association, with players like Albert G. Spalding and second baseman Ross Barnes. Those original cards are incredibly rare and valuable, many thousands of dollars. David colored them with his Crayons, and then we decided we didn't want Mother to know we'd been in her things, so David buried his in the yard. I pretty much forgot the two cards I had until I was around eleven or twelve, when I gave them to a guy at school for his dessert at lunch for a week. I don't know what the Topps 1950s cards of Mickey Mantle and Willie Mays are worth today, but I do know that we significantly reduced our inheritance by stealing all those baseball cards—and definitely the most expensive dessert I've ever had!" He paused for laughter that spread through the group like a gentle wave. "I've never seen that metal box again.

"Though we boys have lived far apart, we were all given an amazing childhood, and David built on that to become a caring adult. He wanted to make a difference in the world, to contribute to something greater than his own well-being—from fresh water in Africa to literacy. He has left a wonderful legacy, a tribute to our parents, and an example of good deeds and good intentions. Godspeed, little brother. I will miss you."

Tim sat down, and Melanie put her hand on his arm. Kevin Jr. and Brad made their way to the front of the assembly. Brad was carrying a guitar.

Kev began, "As the middle son, I could make both my older and younger brothers crazy, but I learned from both of them. We are not a religious family, but I have come to see the touch of a higher power in my life. David's death has shaken us all. My partner Brad and I would like to share a loved reminder that has brought us peace. It was part of a sermon delivered in 1847 by Henry Francis Lyte, a writer and poet who was ordained in the Church of England. Years later it became a hymn. The words may be familiar but are printed out for you under your seats, if anyone wants to follow or sing along."

Abide with me! fast falls the eventide;

The darkness deepens; Lord, with me abide!
When other helpers fail and comforts flee,
Help of the helpless, oh, abide with me.

Swift to its close ebbs out life's little day;
Earth's joys grow dim, its glories pass away;
Change and decay in all around I see;
O Thou who changest not, abide with me.

Come not in terrors, as the King of kings;
But kind and good, with healing in Thy wings:
Tears for all woes, a heart for every plea;
Come, Friend of sinners, thus abide with me.

I need Thy presence every passing hour:
What but Thy grace can foil the tempter's power?
Who like Thyself my guide and stay can be?
Through cloud and sunshine, oh, abide with me.

I fear no foe, with Thee at hand to bless:
Ills have no weight, and tears no bitterness:
Where is death's sting? where, grave, thy victory?
I triumph still, if Thou abide with me.

Kev's voice was strong and clear. Brad accompanied him on the guitar and sang occasional harmony. Many guests joined in. At the end, Brad continued to play a postlude. No one moved.

Chapter Eleven

After the service, Brad approached me with a man I had never seen before. "Theresa, I'd like you to meet my father, Razor. He's up from Maryland and came for the funeral."

"How nice to meet you, and how nice of you to come. Brad is an important part of this family."

A tall man with a firm handshake looked me straight in the eye with a dark intensity. He stooped to accommodate a woman stuck in a wheelchair, and as he bent over, long black curls streaked with gray fell onto his shirt collar and shoulders. He was an older version of Brad, with a big smile and olive skin. His hand felt rough but warm.

"Thank you, Theresa. Brad is quite at home here on the Cape, and I've enjoyed getting to know Kev. They lead a full life."

"Yes, they do," I replied, knowing that things were about to get really full and complicated with a child to raise. Brad looked at me with a smile, perhaps wondering if I was about to spill the beans on a grandchild with this new man on my lawn.

"Where do you live in Maryland?" I continued, wanting to ease Brad's curiosity.

"Well, we lived in Potomac for years, where Brad grew up. His mother and I divorced when he was in college, and I moved to the Eastern Shore, to St. Michaels. Guess I've been there about five years now."

I was doing math in my head. I knew Brad was ten years younger than Kev and was an only child, but I didn't have a much fuller picture of his background.

"Oh, we have friends that recently bought a house there, on the Miles River, and want us to come sailing this fall. We've always lived in Alexandria full time."

"St. Michaels is very popular for sailing."

Before we could continue discussing the delights of living on the Chesapeake Bay or the possibility of my being able to go sailing in a month or so, other guests came up to offer condolences. Several also offered sympathy about my accident. Razor had not mentioned it.

Kevin came and asked to wheel me to the refreshment area. "How are you feeling, Theresa? Is this too much?" "Too much" was losing our son, but Kevin was worried about me, and I knew he wanted to help. We still needed time alone to catch up, but today would be filled with company. My physical and mental state would have to have tending later.

Pushing a wheelchair on bumpy ground was not easy, and Tim immediately appeared and took over. "Easy, Dad, let your strong kids have this duty. Let us help while we're here." Kevin did not resist.

Mattie had done a spectacular job of organizing the food, the flowers, parking behind the house, and the traffic pattern for serving. Even Kev remarked how efficient and calm she was, high praise from a man who juggled many responsibilities at a busy restaurant.

The day remained bright and sunny, with the ocean calm and quiet. Birds squawked above and from the beach, and some guests tossed their shoes in the sand as they ventured along the shoreline in shallow water. A funeral became a social gathering, with new connections and friendship. The music continued into the afternoon with songs that David would have liked, groups that included vocals: Jay-Z and Kanye West's "Watch the Throne," Lady Antebellum with "Need You Now," and the Canadian pop-punk band Marianas Trench. I could recognize only some of the music. I knew that David really liked Lady Gaga and the saxophone solo in "The Edge of Glory." His taste was eclectic, even including Bob Dylan. Many of the younger guests were dancing.

I was under the marquee, enjoying some fruit that I could chew and humming along, when Brad came up with Razor to get drinks.

"It's been a perfect day," Brad said. "Well, perfect for what it is, I mean. I could have chosen a better word."

"I understand, and I agree. I've heard so many funny and wonderful stories about David today. I think we're sending him off with lots of love." I could feel the tears forming, filling my eyes.

Razor reached down for my hand. "I'm so glad that I came."

I did not pull back and let him continue to hold my hand, resting on my lap. "How long will you be here? What are your plans?" I asked.

"Well, I don't want to outstay my welcome. I'm staying with Brad and Kev. I drove up yesterday and will remain on the Cape this week and then continue a road trip around New England. I know I'm way too early for the fall colors, but maybe I'll drop anchor somewhere and enjoy the transition later. I don't need to get back."

"We're having a family dinner here tonight, and I hope you will come. Just our family and David's fiancee's. Please do join us."

"I'm not exactly 'family.'"

"You are Brad's father. That's family. We'll see you at 7:30."

Just then, Kevin arrived to check on me. Guests were beginning to leave. I was tired and in pain.

"Perhaps I could have a little rest on the porch," I said to my anxious husband. He began to push my chair, but Brad immediately took over. We continued on into the house, and Brad lifted me carefully onto a lounge, facing the ocean. Razor put a quilt over me, and I was asleep before I could even thank them.

There is magic in Cape Cod air. It comforts and refreshes. There are hints of fragrance and salt. Sounds carry across the water, mixing with voices and music from unknown sources. I awoke to conversation that seemed to be behind me.

"Melanie, we can't. Not here."

"Don't you want me?"

"Of course I want you. You're making me crazy. I didn't realize you weren't wearing anything under that skirt."

"Tim, I want to be close to you."

"You're already sitting on my lap."

There was shuffling and movement, zipping and heavy breathing.

"Melanie, we should go upstairs."

"Love me, *here.*"

"Someone will see us."

"Everyone's left or busy outside cleaning up. Make love to me."

A panting sound increased, as Tim gave in to the seduction.

Melanie did not slow down: "Pull me into you. Pull me hard. Harder!"

My shy and sometimes awkward son was at the height of pleasure, gasping and moaning. They shared a rhythm of release that got louder. I was listening to a sound track of sex and did not dare move a muscle.

"I want you so much," exclaimed Tim in short breaths.

"Make me pregnant. Make me pregnant now."

I could hear them kissing, exploring. I could easily understand the picture without the visuals. It was like a radio show of lovemaking. Then there was silence.

"Good God, what were we thinking?" Tim said finally. "Your skin is so hot and soft, Melanie. All of you is so smooth; I can't take my hands off you."

I felt like Hercule Poirot in an Agatha Christie novel, hiding behind the tall back of a wing chair, in a study with perpetrators discussing their crime. Tim was both the victim and the perpetrator. The angle of the lounge shielded me from view. I assumed they were making love on one of the chairs at the table, just twenty feet from me. I guess the hurried lovers did not notice an empty wheelchair folded against the wall.

I felt sad for my son, whose life had set limits on him that were not fair. He was stuck in a situation for which society provided few options. He was locked out of real happiness in his marriage and found only a fleeting substitute to help him forget.

Psychological liberty is cold consolation. Tim had found freedom not in love, but in his lust. Perhaps life is just facing a series of problems that need to be sorted out and lined up in order. For Tim, destiny had fallen off track.

I waited for the two lovers to regain their composure and leave the room. How odd and curious it was to be witness to Tim's infidelity. He would be mortified. Sex was the trap that continued to snare him. I could not judge.

For an hour or so, I remained between sleep and awake, sorting through thoughts of David, the accident, and living life with two sons instead of three. I felt a hand on my arm and looked up to see Kevin.

"I didn't mean to wake you."

"It's all right. I've just been coasting, resting my eyes."

"Are you in pain?"

"Yes, but perhaps that's a sign that mending is underway. I feel so foolish, Kevin."

"You've had a dreadful week. Unimaginable. I'm so sorry for what you've had to go through."

"I've been trying to remember, to recreate the accident. I was arguing with David about his marrying Susan, and he couldn't understand why I didn't support him. He was angry. Really angry. He would not accept my suggestion that they wait, to be sure. We had hurried to the subway platform, and it was crowded with rush hour passengers. People were pushing and closing in. David was holding my arm. I was distressed and anxious. And then he was gone. He had fallen in front of the train. Someone screamed, maybe me. People stopped. I can't remember after that."

"Theresa, it was an accident. A terrible, terrible, freak accident."

"But he died thinking I didn't care for him, didn't trust him."

"I'm sure that's not true," Kevin replied and then hesitated. "But why were you so opposed to his marrying Susan? She is a wonderful young woman, and they've known each other forever. Why weren't you thrilled? They were certainly both old enough, neither having married by their mid-thirties." He paused and looked out at the lawn, still strewn with chairs and the look of a party. "I feel so sad for her. She is devastated. She could hardly speak today."

Obviously, there was not a sensible reason I could share. I muttered something about their needing to take their time. It was feeble, even to me.

Kevin did not press. "The hospital has called about your check-up visit. Shall we go now or do it after dinner? They want to be sure you're doing all right."

"I think now would be good. The worst of today is over, and I can be more relaxed. It's just family tonight."

Kevin began to help me up and then stopped, calling for Tim.

"No, no," I said quickly, "let's see if I can't get into the chair myself." I did not want to be found in the auditorium of Tim's intimate performance.

Kevin wheeled me to the bathroom, and then he went to find Tim, the only available strong helper to assist with lifting me into the car. Brad and Kev had left with Razor and would return for dinner. Melanie was helping Mattie set the dining room table.

I was nervous about facing questions and the medical verdict resulting from mental lapse. How could I rationalize what happened?

A nurse gently unwrapped me as I lay once again on a hospital bed. "We'll just change these bandages. Maybe a couple of them can be eliminated, now that the bleeding has slowed."

I liked the thought of looking less like something dug up from a tomb, preserved in linen for the afterlife. "Isn't air good for healing?" I asked.

"Yes, but we need to protect the worst wounds. Some of these lacerations were quite deep. The stitches look good."

"Sit tight, Theresa," Kevin added, sitting down in the only available chair. He looked pale. "Our objective is to keep you home tonight. No arguing."

There were no questions about mental instability, only tips for physical balance and the need to use my cane more regularly. I had passed the first hurdle and could stay at home, with hospital check-ins every two days for a week. Then a visiting nurse could come to the house.

Tim lifted me into the rental car, and he drove, while Kevin and I sat close together in the back. Melanie was waiting in the driveway with my wheelchair. "What's the news?"

"I am released for dinner and safe for overnights at home," I replied. Tim carefully lifted me out, but Kevin remained in the car.

"Are you all right, Kevin?" I asked.

"I'm fine, but I think I'll just sit here a minute. It's been quite a day. I need to catch my breath."

"I'll be right back, Dad."

"No, no. Not to worry."

Melanie and Tim got me into the house, and I asked, "Do you think Dad's okay? He seems not quite himself."

"I'm sure it's just the long day, needing to greet and talk with everyone, remembering David and sharing grief. Mom, I can't even imagine how hard this day was for you and Dad. Melanie and I would like to stay a few extra days to help, if that's all right. She loves it here, and perhaps I can help with the physical stuff. Maybe Dad should be slowing down a little and not doing so much lifting."

"I've noticed that younger muscle keeps stepping forward. Are you not telling me something that I should know?"

"Of course not, but our limits sometimes sneak up on us," Tim answered.

I laughed. "You don't have to tell me! I'm redefining 'limits' every day. And it would be wonderful to have you here as long as you can stay. Having my family together is the best possible solace."

And then, for absolutely no specific reason at all, I burst into tears, sobbing. Melanie took my hand, and my love-starved son got down on his knees next to the wheelchair and cradled me in his arms.

Chapter Twelve

Robert Herrick's famous poem was addressed to virgins, but I think of it as being for anyone who has not fully tasted life. I think of it as an urgent roadmap for youth—and a reminder of the opportunities lost to David. Time passes quickly. We have said goodbye, but parting comes only slowly. Carpe diem.

Gather ye rosebuds while ye may,
 Old time is still a-flying;
And this same flower that smiles today
 Tomorrow will be dying.

The glorious lamp of heaven, the sun,
 The higher he's a-getting,
The sooner will his race be run,
 And nearer he's to setting.

That age is best which is the first,
 When youth and blood are warmer;
But being spent, the worse, and worst
 Times still succeed the former.

Then be not coy, but use your time,
 And, while ye may, go marry;
For, having lost but once your prime,
 You may forever tarry.

Chapter Thirteen

Theodosia's long, white marble dining table is imposing. It clearly provides an invitation to a banquet, a large
gathering of friends, ideas, and conversation. The table
itself is a bold statement—nothing unobtrusive or shy—
but a heavy piece of supported marble that looks as
though it could also hold the weight of tipsy guests who
want to climb up and sermonize or dance and sing. The
early days of Whimsy Towers were lively times under
Theodosia's spell of camaraderie and fun. Her table was
the gathering point. I had never before David's death
thought of the welcoming table as a cold slab in a
morgue, as a call to grief. I did not see David's body after
the accident. It was not a memory to choose.

Ten places were set, with easily room for more.
Mattie had pulled out the best china, elegant silver from
a bygone era, and various cut glasses for wine and water.
Flowers from the garden graced every surface in the
room. Fragrance and candles created an atmosphere of
celebration. Whimsy Towers still liked a party.

I was careful not to seat either of my sons next to
Rick. Similarities were obvious to me, but we see in a
likeness what pleases us. I needed to avoid encouraging
anything that confirmed birthright. Rick's imprint was

clear. The boys were growing more into him; but, luckily, he was gradually aging away from them.

Kevin had helped me get into clothing both workable and appropriate for the evening occasion. My wardrobe choices were limited to fitting over bandages and allowing for arms that didn't fully bend. I felt like a package wrapped for display. Rick's wife and daughter both wore blue, David's favorite color.

Susan looked completely stricken. She was returning to Washington the next day, returning to a life without David, an unexpected and empty future. After the funeral, I had asked if there was anything of David's that she would like to have. I was touched by her answer: "I'd like his Whimsy Towers bathrobe." I'd inherited a house with a dozen enormous fluffy pink towels and terry cloth robes, all embroidered with "Whimsy Towers" in flowing blue letters. As the years went by, I replenished and replaced them as guests or family carried them off. Susan would forever have David wrapped around her in terry cloth pink, with the memory of their lives together in Chatham, at Whimsy Towers. Since she had a key to his D.C. apartment, I told her to go in any time. Kevin and I would deal with settling David's affairs when we returned in a few weeks.

Brad, Kev, and Razor arrived exactly at 7:30. Provincetown is less than an hour's drive, an easy trip that has a change of scenery from the green of Chatham to the sandy roadsides going north. Provincetown is a hub of diversity, art, theater, and exposed bodies in the sunshine. There is whale watching, fishing, and great food.

It is vibrant and exciting; Chatham is more refined and predictable. P-town has glitter; Chatham has diamonds. Both are wonderful.

We all found our places at the table, and I was wheeled between my sons. With everyone seated, Kevin remained standing and began, "This beautiful dinner should have been the engagement party for David and Susan. Our hearts are broken for their lost love as well as for our loss, but we are so grateful to have everyone in this room who is dearest to us. Thank you for sharing in the life of our son, and thank you for sharing in our collective remembering of him. I think we need human connections to deal with grief, to help us regain resilience as we go forward. Tonight, let's give thanks for David."

Glasses clinked, and the dinner proceeded like a play:

ACT ONE

SUSAN: But how do we get over this? Where do I go with my grief? Do I hold it, hide it? Will it heal?

KEVIN: We have to live with loss, but David is part of who we are. There is finality in death but not closure to grief. I think there is no getting over it, ever, and there should not be. In a very obvious sense, we cannot fix what has happened, but there is no closing the door on an emptiness that will fill only slowly.

SUSAN: I just can't let go of him.

Rick puts his arm around his daughter, pulling her close. Conversation pauses.

RICK: We grieve for the times we will not share with David, the events and milestones that will pass without him; but, Susan, you cannot weigh yourself down with rocks so heavy they cannot be lifted.

KEVIN: Does anyone remember the "five stages of grief," popular in the 1960s? I revisited them when Theresa called me in Virginia with the dreadful news. I wanted to examine my own feelings and reaction. Perhaps that's the lawyer in me. But the father needed to understand. Denial, anger, bargaining, depression, acceptance.

RICK: Are you finding them in that order?

KEVIN: I'm sure everyone responds differently, and we cannot judge. My first reaction was self-condemnation.

RICK: But, Kevin, you weren't even there.

KEVIN: No, but you see, I could have changed the whole thing.

Kevin takes a deep breath and looks at Theresa. All motion in the room freezes.

KEVIN: I was here the week before with Theresa. For a surprise, I had gotten tickets to the Broadway show "Hamilton." They were hard to get and we had to wait months, but last week we were going to New York for a belated celebration of our anniversary. At the last minute, I was called back to D.C. for an unscheduled and important meeting. I debated going but felt it was not negotiable. David flew up to accompany his mother to the theater, and we literally passed in the airport. So you see, if I had not left, the accident would not have happened.

THERESA: Oh, Kevin, you cannot blame yourself. We cannot deal with "what if."

The caterers continue to serve, filling glasses and moving around the room.

MELANIE: Sometimes I wonder whether we're looking at the whole picture of life and death in the wrong way. In my graduate program, we recently considered words from Isaiah, "Cease ye from man, whose breath is in his nostrils: for wherein is he to be accounted of?" Looking at over two dozen Bible translations, we found expressions of "stop believing," "don't trust," "turn away from mortals." This human picture is so aggressive and so decisive, but is it the final word? Who is really accountable for it?

KEVIN: I can accept that appearance is not the indicator of the soul, but what do you mean? Life feels very real, and death seems quite final.

MELANIE: I mean that, for Christians, according to Bible scholars, there are two distinct documents about creation in Genesis. They are contradictory. The first is the familiar God creating the heaven and the earth "in His own image," His likeness. The important point is that He saw everything that he had made, "and behold, it was very good." Not just okay or sometimes good and sometimes bad, but "very good." Creation was finished. Then up comes the mist in Chapter 2, clouding this version of creation and making a couple of disobedient humans and a sneaky snake.

The first understanding of creation is done by God as Elohim. The next version is by God, Jehovah. One is wholly spiritual, and the other is material. You really cannot have or believe both. I think Christianity has an edge on this discussion with the example of Christ Jesus. He did not accept illness, death, or anything opposed to the spiritual image of man, the first account of creation. He didn't settle for the material picture; he healed it.

Death is a passage of mortality and a difficult and painful adjustment, but is it the end? Do the molecules of our bodies have intelligence or life? If you cut me open, will you find life?

THERESA: When I received David's ashes this morning, I struggled to understand just where he is now. To me he is as real as Middle C on the piano. Can he be finished? He is an idea that will remain. I cannot see him any more than I can see motherhood or love. Perhaps that's glimpsing his eternal identity.

MELANIE: I guess I like to think that David, all of us really, is inseparable from our loving creator, that life actually exists before as well as after what we see and call birth and death. Life as consciousness, not bodies.

SUSAN: But I cannot hold him.

MELANIE: No, but you will always have opportunities to express love—and to receive it.

KEVIN: I think we are all trying to grasp the bigger meaning here, to make sense of the senseless. Perhaps getting out of the Garden of Eden is the first step!

Candles flicker with increased intensity as the room darkens, shedding more light on the paintings on the walls. They seem to come in closer. Guests look thoughtful.

RAZOR: I am new to the gathering of this family, and I never met David, but earlier today, I heard an astounding amount of heartfelt tributes to him. I do not know if the present is just a time of preparation for the future or a respite from it, but today is all we can know. David touched many people. I cannot help but think of Welsh ploughmen in medieval times who walked backwards in front of their oxen, singing to them as they worked in the fields. I'd like to think of David as singing to *us*, reminding us to go forward with joy, with a rhythm and determination that both comforts and encourages.

THERESA: That's a beautiful idea. Thank you for sharing it.

Kev and Brad clasp hands on the table.

KEV: Well, we have some good, going forward news. Brad and I have begun the process of adopting a baby boy.

All eyes turn. Glasses are raised.

RAZOR: That's fantastic news! Congratulations!

BRAD: We're in early days but feel optimistic. And we'd like permission to have "David" be his middle name. We will hyphenate our last names, but we didn't want you to think we were trying to replace David in any way.

THERESA: I think that's a wonderful tribute. What do you think, Kevin?

KEVIN: A very touching gesture. I mean it, I think that's great. David would be pleased. How do you proceed? Do we need to gear up for some positive referrals or interviews? Do we need coaching?

Laughter.

KEV: You've spent too much time in court, Dad. Maybe we'll tell them we have no family at all! Then the little guy can begin life with only one generation of mistakes to live down!

BRAD: This is a big chapter in our life. Everyone at this table knows of our commitment and love. We're really excited.

Kev stands up.

KEV: I think this is the perfect time and place and in front of our family. Brad, you are my forever partner. I'd like us to begin as parents as a married couple. Will you marry me?

Brad stands, and the two men embrace. Applause.

BRAD: Of course I will. I cannot see my life without you.

TIM: Goodness, this brings some good news to the table—and another excuse to come back to Chatham. Well done! You are proof that the world doesn't stop for our pain.

Glasses are raised. Melanie looks down.

THERESA: How wonderful to celebrate a marriage, but I hope no one ever needs an excuse to come here. Tim, I wish that we might see you more than once a year, either here or in Virginia. Whimsy Towers exists to be used. It's in the DNA. And that includes you, too, Razor. Please know that you are always welcome here. Maybe, when there is 24/7 baby noise, you would like an intermission when you visit!

RAZOR: Thank you, Theresa, I will keep that in mind. I've felt very welcomed already. I see that our families are being pulled closer together, and I'm glad.

TIM: And speaking of DNA, David thought it would be fun to chart our family's DNA, to find out our ancestral heritage. Are we descended from cave dwellers? Are you and Dad distant cousins, like British royalty in the days of incest and madness?

I recently saw a documentary called "Three Identical Strangers." It was about triplets all separated at birth and adopted. Imagine meeting someone as an adult who is yourself in a mirror? Their family history had been torn from them, and it was sad and sobering to think they didn't know where they had belonged or even that they had biological siblings. They were raised with lies.

David began the DNA process at home, with a company in D.C., but I don't know who or the status of the results. I guess there's no way to follow up now, unless you find mail in his apartment. Maybe we should begin again, while we're all here to give samples.

Theresa gasps, coughing.

KEV: Mother, are you all right? You look as though you've seen a ghost.

THERESA: I don't think I want to see the ghosts of my past. I'm happy with the family connections in this room, thank you. Every generation turns a new page; the old ones can stay behind. Let's not disturb the dust.

KEV: Afraid of skeletons?

THERESA: Afraid you will find out we're related to some horrible revolutionary on the wrong side of history. And your child is beginning a new resume. Don't tie him to something that excludes him.

KEV: Perhaps you've got a point.

THERESA: Truth is, we create family more than inherit it.

KEVIN: I'll drink to that. And to the family at this table.

General, unintelligible conversation, toasting, and animation.

RAZOR: I was interested to learn at the funeral about your family's mother-son trips and David's resulting interest in Africa. Where did you go, Kev?

KEV: I was struggling with French in high school, so off we went to France. We did a bike trip in the countryside around Provence. It was quite a deluxe vacation, designed for parents and teenagers. We stayed in castles and had great food. Every comfort and service was provided. The biking was really good, and the group was fun.

RAZOR: And did your French improve?

KEV: I'm not sure, but I did a taste test of chocolate croissants in every village, lost my virginity in a barn in the rain, and developed an interest in French cuisine and cooking.

RAZOR: Sounds like a most successful vacation! And you, Tim?

TIM: Mother and I went to the Middle East and northern Africa. It was an ambitious undertaking. In Morocco we rode camels for several hours out into the Sahara Desert to a large tent hung with Oriental carpets and carpets laid directly on the sand, where we sat to eat. After settling in, I decided to drag my bedding outside and ended up sleeping under the stars in front of the fire, still giving off light and sparks. I will never forget that expanse of sky in the desert.

The other best memory was visiting Petra, in the southern Jordan desert. It's an archaeological city carved into a sandstone hill in the first century BC. The most amazing part is the rose-red façade of the breathtaking Treasury building. The original function is still a mystery, but the columns with Corinthian capitals, friezes, and royal tomb elements showcase the possibilities of the Nabataean caravan city, most of which is still undiscovered underground. If you saw the movie "Indiana Jones and the Last Crusade," you saw Harrison Ford coming upon Petra! It was actually discovered by outsiders only in the 1800s, by a European traveler who disguised himself as a Bedouin to gain access. Check out the movie—or Google Petra. You won't believe it.

RAZOR: Sounds like two vacations that have left a lasting impact. What a good idea, Theresa.

THERESA: Yes, but the trips were also good for me, too. I had an opportunity to spend time with the boys in a way a mother cannot normally have with sons—even before the days of regular cell phones and Facebook pages! They were all mine. I had not traveled growing up, so I wanted my children to have a more expansive view of the world. Disney World was a great family trip when they were little, but I wanted some cultural influence by the time they were teenagers, and I wanted to experience it with them one on one.

KEVIN: And I came to appreciate Theresa even more after two weeks on my own with whoever was left at home!

TIM: I've never had a vacation outside the country since. Guess that one will have to last me, but it definitely stirred my interest in history and architecture.

Conversation breaks off into smaller groups.

THERESA: Where's the silver cup?

TIM: What cup?

THERESA: My mother's baby cup. It's always in this room, over there.

KEVIN: Maybe the caterers moved it.

Servers stop.

KEVIN: Have you seen a small silver cup?

CATERER 1: No, sir, but I can check with the others. Things were moved around a bit to accommodate the flowers.

KEVIN: Of course, thank you. By the way, this meal is spectacular, and everything at the funeral reception was very well done. You've helped us a great deal.

CATERER 1: Thank you, sir.

THERESA: And look, several of the Herend figurines are missing on the top shelf! Two of the rabbits and the sleigh are gone. And the kaleidoscope turtle, which is the most valuable of the collection! What's going on?

TIM: I'm sorry to say it, Mother, but there were a lot of people here today, and many we did not know. They came and went in the house, using the bathroom and probably following their curiosity around. Small items can be tempting souvenirs.

THERESA: I can't believe that anyone who cared about David would steal from us.

KEV: Please don't get agitated. You'll split your stitches. We can't do anything at this moment. Try to relax and enjoy your dinner. This clam chowder is delicious. I want to ask them later about the seasoning. I can't quite put my finger on it. Can you tell, Brad?

BRAD: No, but it's a serious challenger to ours. Really good.

THERESA: And the beehive is gone!

TIM: Mother, stop.

An uncomfortable silence settles on the party. Furtive glances. Servers begin to pick up the soup plates as others bring in the main course.

RICK: Well, I'd like to propose a toast: To our longtime family friends. May you find strength in the grief of this moment. May you find joy in knowing that you created and brought up an exceptional young man. May David's memory continue to inspire us all.

Theresa weeps openly in her wheelchair, as everyone stands. Rick raises his glass toward the urn on the side table.

KEVIN: Thank you, Rick. I know you loved him like a son. Let's all continue to focus on his life, not the picture of his death.

Theresa lowers her head into her hands, trembling, as glasses clink.

THERESA: Oh, my God. I pushed him. I pushed him!

KEVIN: What, Theresa? What did you say?

THERESA: I.... I.... I rushed him. I rushed him at the subway.

KEVIN: There is no blame, Theresa. David had an accident.

Chapter Fourteen

The rest of the dinner was a blur, until I heard an eerie melody coming from the kitchen, a haunting, magnetic song:

> *Amazing grace! How sweet the sound*
> *That saved a wretch like me!*
> *I once was lost, but now am found;*
> *Was blind, but now I see.*

Conversation stopped, and we all turned to see Mattie coming into the dining room, carrying her apple stack cake. She stood next to Kevin and me and continued singing in her soft, southern way:

> *Through many dangers, toils and snares,*
> *I have already come;*
> *'Tis grace hath brought me safe thus far,*
> *And grace will lead me home.*
>
> *The Lord has promised good to me,*
> *His Word my hope secures;*
> *He will my Shield and Portion be,*
> *As long as life endures.*
>
> *Yea, when this flesh and heart shall fail,*

And mortal life shall cease,
I shall possess, within the veil,
A life of joy and peace.

The earth shall soon dissolve like snow,
The sun forbear to shine;
But God, who called me here below,
Will be forever mine.

When we've been there ten thousand years,
Bright shining as the sun,
We've no less days to sing God's praise
Than when we'd first begun.

Different words have been incorporated over the several hundred years of John Newton's "Amazing Grace," but I have never heard a more profound or moving rendition. It was Mattie's gift to us of inspiration and praise, of hope for renewal.

Mattie is the niece of Bessie, a woman who had worked for Elizabeth's parents in South Carolina. Her family has seen more than their share of alcoholism and drug problems. Mattie knows the sadness of death and loss, but she is ever the optimist. She held us spellbound as she sang, holding her five-layer offering of love. She lifted our spirits to a place of serenity.

Incremental dying must be easier to deal with. The hot breath of death exhales slowly when a loved one is ill, but blows without restraint after an accident. The effect of a 19th century letter with black-edged envelope is the same in every generation. Death has called. Mourning begins.

Not long ago, a large airliner was lost at sea. Hundreds of people and the plane are still missing. Those who mourn their loved ones must deal with unresolved loss. I don't like unanswered questions. We can put identification chips in our dogs but cannot locate an off-course and downed airplane. The uncertainty of life is a reminder to live it.

My mother and grandmother left without goodbye. David, too, left without goodbye, and now I remember that I might have been the instrument of his death. The horror of that moment has become clearer. I was agitated and angry, frustrated with how to deal with his desire to marry Susan. Fury roared. I remember pushing him. I pushed my son into silence, into oblivion. He can never have the expectation of tomorrow, and I will never have the peace of it. I have done the unimaginable. I am not beyond the reach of madness.

Is it possible that I caused David's death? Memory is convincing. Sometimes I feel I am here and not here at the same time, like looking into a mirror that doesn't look back. I cannot see a future. I cannot see how to atone. Is remembering enough punishment? Dare I speak of it? Would my admission ease anyone's burden?

When the dinner ended and everyone hugged good night, I wanted to leap from my wheelchair and hold my two sons close. I wanted to reinforce my love for them; I wanted to feel their limbs alive. I wanted not to be a murderer.

We decided that Kevin and I could share a bed without doing damage to my injuries, and Kev and Tim carried me upstairs. I did not want to be without the man who for half a century had fallen asleep holding my hand. The business of undressing and bathing and redressing was laborious and exhausting. Kevin patiently lifted the nightgown over my head and arms, careful not to bump the bandages. We could not easily hold each other physically, but we shared memories of our lost son. Together we cried tears of gratitude and sorrow, and I cried tears of remorse and guilt. We talked of what to do with David's ashes, when to clean out his apartment, and how to shift our world without him.

Mornings come early in a room without shades or curtains. I have never wanted to block the announcement of the sun rising from the ocean, making known its arrival in bright light across the room. Noisy birds share in the good news of another day as they roost and nest just outside the window. Branches scratch against the glass.

The ocean does not stop its tidal rush to shore, no matter what develops on land. The ocean is the constant at Whimsy Towers. It does not notice that the past is outmoded or if the future is cloudy. Every season brings fresh breezes into the house, and we close the windows only when the rain insists.

I awoke to the realization that I could not turn my body. My legs hurt, and blood had oozed onto the sheets through a bandage. I tried to slide over a little. Kevin had strayed close to the edge of the bed, probably hoping to keep me safe.

"Kevin, are you awake? Can you help me to the bathroom?"

There was no answer. I tried again.

"I'm so sorry, but I need help getting to the bathroom."

Still he did not answer, and I reached over to touch him.

ങ

"Tim! Tim! Help! Please help me! Someone, help!"

Mattie was the first to arrive. She had not even bothered to cover her pajamas but burst into the room as if there were a fire. "What is it? What's the matter?"

Tim was right behind her.

"Oh, Tim, it's your father! He isn't moving, and he's cold. *So* cold."

Tim hurried to the far bedside, picking up Kevin's hand, with a stricken look on his face. He touched his father's cheek. "He's gone. Mother, he's gone."

Melanie appeared in the doorway, and everyone froze in disbelief.

"No, it can't be!" I wailed, breaking the stillness. "No, Kevin, don't leave me! Please don't leave me."

I couldn't move my body to get close to him. I was helpless. Kevin had been lifted from earthbound limits, and I was mired in them.

"I need to call Kev," Tim said, as he passed Melanie and Mattie and left the room. "I'll be right back," he called from the hall. "We'll take care of this."

Tim returned with his phone and called his brother. His voice cracked as he explained what had happened. "No, no warning. He just didn't wake up. Get here as soon as you can."

Tim debated covering Kevin's face and then pulled the sheet over him, putting his father in the dark. We four stayed in the sunny bedroom, still painted yellow from Theodosia's time. The day began in a way no one could have predicted. Life and death waited together. I didn't want to leave Kevin alone.

Mattie and Melanie helped me to the bathroom and to dress. We moved in silence. More than a dead body was in that room. I felt the death of hope, of purpose. I can't bear another funeral and letting go of our shared memories. I have never been without Kevin. We stepped into each other's lives in college and finally found one that fit us both. Now I would need to move on without him.

Kev arrived with Brad and Razor. Kev came first to me and then to check his father, lying on the bed as if still asleep. He replaced the sheet and said, "I'm so sorry, Mom. I'm so sorry."

I refused to leave the room until Kevin was taken away. Tim put me in a chair next to Kevin, and I held his lifeless hand on the bed. My husband of fifty years lay calm and alone. Mattie brought coffee and biscuits. The boys made arrangements. Razor and Melanie stayed in the background.

"He didn't want you to know," Kev began. "He made us promise."

"Promise what? What are you talking about?"

"Dad was sick. He had a heart condition, Mother, and he didn't want to worry you."

"Worry me?"

"He'd had some tests. The reason he didn't go to New York with you was that the heart specialist he was waiting to see in D.C. had a cancellation. Dad thought it was important to go. Do you really think he would have skipped out on you for an office meeting?"

"While you spent the night in the hospital," Tim continued, "he told us everything over dinner and asked us to witness a codicil to his will that he brought from home. He especially didn't want to burden you with everything else going on. I don't think he thought anything was imminent, but he was told to take things a little easier."

"You darling man," I said aloud, gently squeezing the cool hand. "You should have told me." Tears slipped down my face, and I hardly noticed.

"He wanted to protect you, Mother; that was his nature, but he especially hated the idea that he was creating a secret between you. It troubled him a great deal that he wasn't being honest with you, that he was withholding something so important. It hurt a lot to live with that, and now he's died with it. Please forgive him."

I looked at my two sons, realizing how I have been able to compartmentalize lies. "I have much more to be

forgiven, much more. How like your father to slip away without bother, not to inconvenience anyone."

We sat quietly for a few minutes, and then I asked, "What's in the codicil?"

"Dad saw how difficult David's death and funeral preparations have been. He requested no funeral service and that his ashes be placed with yours, whenever the time comes, if he went first." Tim tried to laugh. "He wanted to be wherever you're going! He always wanted to be next to you. He loved your life together."

I don't do well in a perfectly defined world. I have rebelled against convention, against other people's idea of proper behavior and expectation. I have deceived and maneuvered those I love. I have defied the rules that my husband valued.

ᏨᎦ

"How do we go forward?" I asked no one in particular, as a black van drove off, and we were left outside on the patio. I wanted to be out of the wheelchair, chasing after the life that had been taken from me. I could hear ocean waves rolling in, insistent and familiar, reminding me that life is more than just believing and accepting the repetition of what we know. New beginnings would require persistence and the tenacity not to be deterred. Changes were coming.

"Well, our first need, Mother, is figuring out your living situation. Even when you can walk again, you cannot live here or in Virginia on your own—at least not until you're more consistently stable. We need to face facts. Perhaps Mattie would consider staying with you year-round. Her family arrangement in South Carolina seems pretty casual. Do you think you'll want to maintain both houses?"

"It's too early to say. And I have David's place to clean out."

Razor spoke up, "I can help you with that, Theresa, if you'd like. I'm not that far from D.C. My work is all volunteer, so I'm flexible on time. I'd be so glad to help, if you'd allow me. Both your boys are pretty far away."

"That's really kind, Dad," Brad answered. "I wish we were not so far from Virginia, but we can do a better job of checking in here on the Cape. And, hopefully, we'll have an active little one to bring around and show off!"

"Yes, Razor, thank you," I added. "I would definitely be glad for the help. I know Kevin's office will deal with legal details, but the apartment needs to be cleared out. Oh, Tim, we need to call Dad's office."

"Already done, Mother. They'll be in touch."

Mattie announced that lunch was ready and that she would be bringing it outside. The sun had risen to its noonday height, spreading warmth indiscriminately on all. No one suggested rolling out the large, striped awning that would bring shade and cover. We wanted the sunshine.

Chapter Fifteen

The right whales off Cape Cod are drastically reduced in number. They are changing their migration patterns. With less plankton to eat in the increasingly warming waters, they are going farther north for food. I wonder whether they miss what they are used to, whether they regret the changes or simply make them. Food, shelter, love. Is all of life just a series of variation on the search for these? Until now, they have been steady in my life, but food, shelter, and love can take differing forms.

We are created by what's gone before, but I am trying to see where the future may lead. I confess to a fear of losing the familiar, of holding on to what cannot remain. In the few months since Kevin's death, I have made some choices. Being able to walk again has also brought renewed strength and grit. I need to do battle with physical and mental decline.

Razor drove me to Virginia, where he stayed in Alexandria at my house, while we cleaned out David's apartment in Washington. A long day in the car driving south provided lots of opportunity for conversation, and Razor was easy company.

I had not yet been able to tell Kevin, but while I was in the hospital, a neurologist came to see me on his rounds. We talked about cognitive abilities and how to work around deficiencies. He explained how the brain can be altered, that it's not fixed. We adapt, simplify, and accommodate. It is possible, even necessary, to build brain health.

Razor had listened attentively and then said simply, "So, you need to challenge your brain!"

He had summarized it perfectly. I needed to challenge myself to learn new skills, to have more social interaction, to problem solve. Resting in decline was no longer an option. Resisting was the new mantra. I would not hide in the belief of aging.

I like the idea that I'm in charge, that I have the ability to make change. I would no longer accept the possibility that I could be overwhelmed, that I was a victim of society's collective beliefs. Purposeful engagement was the new strategy.

I could not make an old body a young body, but I could make a stronger body by increased exercise and good diet. Razor took walks with me, increasing in length, often repeating the route I had run many years ago with my dog Gypsy. Razor loved to cook, which did not surprise me, having known his son Brad. He encouraged and pushed me to build a new life, but there was no shaking the horror of David's accident. Should I conceal the truth? For two weeks in Virginia, we dealt with David's apartment in D.C., cleaned out closets, raked leaves, and talked of life and relationships in front of the fire.

Learning new things requires mental engagement and focus, and I was trying to create new outlines for living my life. Losing two men I loved made me stumble going forward, but fear of consequences produces reticence and is self-limiting. I needed a targeted approach to avoid distraction, and Razor was my coach and cheerleader. He helped me concentrate on life, not death.

One morning at breakfast, the house phone rang. "Today's the day!" boomed Kev. "We pick up our son today!"

The wonderful news was the signal to return to Chatham. It was time. My work was finished, and I wanted to be at Whimsy Towers for Thanksgiving.

"What are your plans, Razor? Will you come back to the Cape? There is no pressure; I can certainly fly back. We do, however, have a new grandson to meet!"

"I would be glad to return with you," he answered. "I've enjoyed our time together here, and maybe there are things I can help you with at Whimsy Towers."

"Sounds perfect. We'll meet the heir to the throne together!"

If Razor found it awkward or embarrassing to help me clean out Kevin's things, he showed no sign of it. I wanted to keep all the photos and personal memorabilia that decorated tables and walls, but I felt it was macabre to hold onto his clothes and toiletries. Digging into death is invasive, and I wanted it to pass.

There were many tears during those several weeks as I came across items that triggered memories. Razor was patient, respectful, but he urged me on. Without his help, I would have been swallowed up or just avoided the whole process. It is cathartic to unload unnecessary stuff, and my initial feeling of disloyalty slowly dissolved. I made a pile of things the boys might like: Kevin's baseball glove, his mostly unused golf clubs, some ties, a model airplane he'd made as a child. Only David still had belongings in the house, and now there was no need to keep them either. The thrift store became a regular stop on the way to Chinese dinner or a stroll along the riverfront in Old Town.

I showed Razor around my adopted hometown, especially the historic part that has streets lined with imposing red brick houses and shops. Robert E. Lee, George Washington, even Lafayette have left their mark. Washington was a surveyor there early in his career and later kept a house in town for when he couldn't make the long, arduous, ten-mile trip back to Mt. Vernon. Now a bike path runs the whole distance along the Potomac River.

In the middle of a busy intersection stands a tall Confederate soldier statue, facing south. Alexandria has slave history, but the controversy about removing offensive statues has not budged the remnants of southern pride there. Some people do not want to challenge history, some want to re-interpret it, and some want to expunge painful memories altogether. I wonder if personal family histories can be as complex in how we acknowledge their lasting impact. One day my mistakes will ultimately come to light. My secrets will surface through science or confrontation and tarnish the family name. I hope I will be beyond reach, like a bird that disappears in flight.

Alexandria held onto autumn colors longer than the Cape, and the days were warmer. Razor had taken many weeks after the funeral to explore New England and to anticipate the change of season, but the reds and yellows were still strong as we drove south together, once the doctors had proclaimed me fit to travel. We planned to return in mid-November for the first blush of northeast winter. I have never stayed at Whimsy Towers past Thanksgiving and wondered how winter would be. Mattie had agreed to come back as full-time house-keeper, which eased the minds of my sons, so I felt I had options living on my own.

Before we left Virginia, Razor took me for a day to St. Michaels, Maryland, where he lived. In less than two hours, we were sitting outside on a clear fall day at the harbor, eating crab cakes with coleslaw and onion rings. Sailboats were docked all around the marina, and visiting boats of varying kinds and sizes tied up at The Crab Claw, so the owners and crew could step out for lunch. Ducks swam close by.

"How did you end up here?" I asked. "It's a beautiful little town."

"It's a simple story, really. When my marriage broke up, I retired from my job and wanted a fresh start. I guess divorce and death both make that demand. I had always enjoyed working with my hands, and I came here and asked if I could volunteer at the maritime museum in the boatyard, which is right next door. And so I've been do-ing wooden boat restoration these last few years, trying to keep the historic old girls seaworthy. I learn and I teach. It's been great."

"I've never heard what you did before this, in your previous life, when Brad was growing up."

He hesitated. "I worked in intelligence. It was hard on the marriage, but not what finally broke it up."

I wasn't sure whether I should ask or let it go. I asked.

"I was with the CIA, Theresa. I speak four languages, including Arabic. I've traveled all over the world, seen a lot. When Brad was in college, he came out to us, announcing he was gay. My wife couldn't handle it. The news disrupted her lifestyle, her family image. She took it as an insult to her ability as a mother. She saw only failure. We argued and argued about it. Finally, there was no going forward for us. We were broken. I quit my job and left. We were all right financially, and when Brad finished school, he headed straight for Cape Cod. He met Kev in Provincetown, and I'm so happy for them. And I feel rather like the legendary bird Phoenix from mythology, rising from the ashes, myself. I think life recycles, if we're paying attention."

"Okay, I finally have to ask. What's the story of your name? It must be good."

Razor smiled. "You know how that works. Now that you're aware of my history, if I tell you, I'll have to kill you." His dark eyes had laughter in them. "It actually is related to my work, cutting through complex problems, I guess—the 'sharper than a razor' thing, perhaps unwilling to be deterred. Intelligence is an intense business. A colleague at Langley gave me the nickname, and it stuck. My real name is Harold. Which do you prefer?"

"I think I'll just stay with Razor! I like it."

I knew that Brad was a lot younger than Kev, and I assumed Razor was at least ten years younger than I, but I was so grateful that these two interesting men had found their way into my family. I was beginning to feel that I, too, was rising from the ashes, not that I had escaped my own death pyre, but because I could see new possibilities for life after devastation and grief. I could not bring back either David or Kevin, but the upheaval and sadness of the summer did not need to overtake the path forward. Crab cakes, sunshine, and good conversation were ingredients of a perfect day.

"Thank you, Razor. I mean it; you've been an incredible help to me. I doubt I could have begun the clearing out of my life, physically or emotionally, if you had not come to help me. I really appreciate it. And you've been my resident brain doctor, helping me not to quit! I spend too much time alone, writing and illustrating; I forget the need to pursue a strong social network to stay brain healthy, to be alert. Kevin and I were just beginning to spend more time together as he eased into retirement. Without the boys around, we had withdrawn into our own bubbles of engagement and interest. We were not unhappy, just programmed."

Razor looked out toward the Miles River, with its broad expanse of blue and gentle tide. Buoys bounced in the current, waiting for boats that needed a firm anchor in the harbor. "I've been thinking about some of the things Melanie was talking about at the dinner for David, about what we accept as identity, about what governs us. I think Kevin hit it perfectly when he suggested the need to get out of the Garden of Eden! We all need to stop limiting ourselves and believing the 'sinner' thing. Our purpose cannot be so limited. And have you ever seen a talking snake? Why should we accept a mortal picture that cannot possibly be from a loving creator? We can do better. Self-fulfilling doom is a snake bite."

I realized that I was gradually feeling stronger physically and mentally—what the neurologist would call "cognitive rewards" from walking, lifting, carrying, analyzing, challenging my limits. In just a few weeks, I had shifted my thought, leaving behind outgrown beliefs of material aging and limitation. Introducing new behavior was more than wishful thinking; it was reorientation. Garden of Eden identity would no longer define me: "for wherein is he to be accounted of?" We have a choice where our thinking goes. I was calling upon a reservoir of latent ability and strength. I stopped limiting myself, stopped avoiding what may be dangerous. Fear was the roadblock. I was quite literally remaking myself into a new person, a new version of possibilities. My history was still following me, but it was not leading the way.

"I think we older people like sympathy," I said. "We get used to the attention that vulnerability provides. We are noticed."

"Are you serious? Older than what? I don't picture you in the 'old' category. Hopefully, you are only older than what is outgrown."

"Well, that's what I'm trying to build on. Pushing aside regret is part of it."

"Theresa, you have some baggage that needs checking."

We both laughed.

"I'm not sure we appear to others the way we see ourselves. And maybe that's a good thing," I said. Only I laughed.

"Would you like to walk around a bit before we have to leave?" asked Razor.

"May I see where you work?"

"Can you jump that fence?"

I looked across at the mischievous man with long hair and dark eyes that could pierce or tease. "If you give me a leg up!"

My new optimism had not gone totally off the rails. I still carried my cane, needing to be aware of unexpected bumpy surfaces. My balance, however, did feel more regular, and my confidence was improving. What I couldn't gauge was whether I was more consistent mentally. I think others need to judge.

Leaving the outdoor restaurant seating, we were literally at the gate of the Chesapeake Bay Maritime Museum. Razor flashed a badge, and we were in, walking toward several buildings used for woodworking and restoration. Inside smelled of freshly-cut wood. Tools hung on the walls, and sawdust and bits of discarded lumber were proof that activity was underway. The resident cat came up to greet us, rubbing against my leg.

"Now there's a thought," I said, "I think I could handle a cat in my life now—or maybe an old dog!"

Building a twenty-five-foot boat was in progress. It rested on a frame several feet off the ground, and I couldn't help rubbing my hand across the smooth surface of the bow. The boat created by long hours of hard labor and precision work was a project for area youth. Razor explained how it was taking shape: the design and sanding, caulking, oiling the floorboards. Young people were learning maritime skills that are slipping away. The legacy of famous boat builders on the Chesapeake Bay was being rekindled in the museum's apprentice program, and the public is invited to watch every step. I was surprised and delighted to learn that a woman was in charge of shipyard programs.

I have always been drawn to men not intimidated by women. Perhaps Theodosia injected that in my blood. Grandmother could not stay in South Carolina with a man who wanted to control her, and she found in Stormy a man who respected her vitality and independence. She was a butterfly he did not try to repaint. He wasn't threatened by the woman he loved; he wanted her to shine. Kevin, too, encouraged my pursuits. We struggled with communication, but I did not doubt his desire to be equal partners as our marriage ripened.

Razor and I walked across Honeymoon Bridge in the marina to the few blocks of downtown St. Michaels. It reminded me a lot of Chatham, with the tourists, ice cream, charming shops, and beckoning restaurants. Even the architecture had similarities. There were modest frame homes and grander ones set in deep gardens. Many had front porches, with plants and wicker furniture loaded with cushions. Trees still touched with hints of autumn yellow lined most of the streets. Brick sidewalks were irregular, and I was glad for Razor's arm. We strolled to the house he rented nearby, where he picked up some additional clothes to take north. I think men don't surround themselves with memories and mementos the way women do. He had few pictures or pieces of furniture, but the rooms were tidy. Perhaps he lived there but didn't yet have a life there.

I learned that St. Michaels, on the Eastern Shore of the Chesapeake Bay, had been a major shipbuilding town when the British roared up the river in the Battle of 1812 to damage the shipyards. Legend says that a young boy suggested that the townspeople hang lanterns in the trees and on boat masts, and that night, the British cannon fire overshot the town. Delightful stories are part of collective imagination and lore. St. Michaels survives on its present ability to welcome visitors to a Chesapeake Bay experience, a ride on an original skipjack, to pick steamed Maryland blue crabs caught that very morning, and to learn about Frederick Douglass, the famous abolitionist and former slave from St. Michaels.

An accomplished and affluent Frederick Douglass returned to St. Michaels after forty-one years to reconcile with his former master, who perhaps was even his father. History carries secrets, and carrying different kinds of grief is a strong temptation. The suggestion that we are blown about by the winds and whims of death and regret is persistent. History is fraught with injustice.

Chapter Sixteen

While cleaning out cupboards in Alexandria, I came across the metal box that Tim had talked about at David's funeral. It was in my father's things when Kevin and I emptied his house after his death. I had not thought of it in years, but I laughed when I saw the remaining baseball cards in the box. Neither Tim nor David had ever told us the story of the purloined cards. They left the 1871-1872 Harry C. Schafer and Harry Wright cards from the Boston Red Stockings. I could picture little David coloring the other old cards to make them pretty for me. He always wanted to see people happy. David wanted to improve the world, even as a young child.

Also still in the box were Topps cards of Sandy Koufax and Al Kaline from the mid-1950s. My father's prized possessions were tampered with by grandchildren he never even got to know and love—and, hopefully, forgive. And he couldn't share the joy of seeing another generation inherit his family's valuable collection. "I forgive you, David," I whispered to myself. "I forgive you both." And then I wondered who could ever forgive *me*.

There were legal papers in the box, but the most important thing was a long, handwritten letter. In it, my father left me information about my mother's accident when I was two and the news that I would inherit my grandmother's house upon his death. His letter changed everything about the future. His silence had left unanswered questions.

I knew only that Mother had died in a sailing accident. My devastated father never could talk about it with Kevin and me, but his letter gave more context. He was a skilled writer, another gift he left his only child. He wrote, in part:

> Storms are not uncommon off the coast of Cape Cod. Winds howl up the rugged coast, gathering trees and chunks of shoreline in their erratic dance of power. Nature has the last word on who or what survives its whims, and your mother loved the challenge of the contest.
>
> Late September is an exciting time for sailing. The summer residents are gone, and the open sea churns with shifts in current and wind. Your mother could not resist racing with the wild, daring the sails to pull her across the breaking waves. The sea spray, the lunging boat with straining keel pounding through the water, and the prospect of a day without destination were thrilling to her.
>
> But the storm was the winner the afternoon she did not come back. An offshore hurricane made an unexpected turn toward land....

She was never found.

I am descended from women who dare. Their voices are silent to me but are like a neume, the sign used in medieval church sheet music indicating direction of melody, the manner of performance, etc. The voices of history are a guide.

Strong women do not fade away; they leave an imprint that is deep. Bold and sassy women do not wear polite masks.

I debated whether I should leave a letter for Tim and Kev about Rick in a secret place or added to the metal box of papers. I wondered whether I could ever tell my story, admit my lack of sexual restraint and the consequences. Dishonesty is only safe in the dark. I must keep hiding in my shame. Confessing to deception as a wife and mother paled in comparison to the possibility that I had caused the death of my own child. I could not do it. The past will have to find its own way into the future.

The last day in Alexandria before driving back to Chatham with Razor brought an odd feeling. I wasn't sure whether I was leaving home or going home. Neither place would be the same without Kevin, and figuring out a life on my own was the unavoidable challenge ahead.

I found an old baby quilt that had been mine and wrapped it for my new grandson. Curiously, it had boats on it. Different colored balloons, puppies, and sailboats floated over the surface in bright appliquéd blues, yellow, and green. No pink to betray a girl baby. I do not know who made it, and it has been tucked away for so many decades, carefully folded in tissue and in excellent condition. An accidental heirloom. My own boys had rougher covers, and I was not clever with a needle.

Razor and I agreed that we would see what the new parents might need and then do some baby shopping together on the Cape. My father had not seen his grandchildren, and Kevin would not see his. I did not ask if Brad's mother would want to know.

"Razor, have you heard the baby's name? I forgot to ask when Kev called."

"I have no idea. Shall we make some guesses?"

"I think it will be very traditional, nothing experimental. And we know his middle name is 'David,' so what works well with that?"

"Anthony David. Jeremy David. William?"

We both laughed, and Razor continued, "I can play this all day! I think boy names are easier than girls'."

"Let's call and see how week one is going. I'm sure we have two sleepless sons!"

I called Kev's cell, and he answered on the fourth ring.

"How's it going up there? We've just been thinking about you," I said. "We'll be back up late tomorrow. Need reinforcements?"

"Hi, Mom. We're trying to figure this out as we go!" Kev answered. "I can't see how anyone can prepare."

I could hear crying in the background. "I don't want to keep you, but we forgot to ask his name."

"We decided on Charles David. What do you think?"

"I think that sounds great. Give Charles David a kiss from us, and we'll see you soon."

I guess the "us" would be his only grandparents, at least the only ones ready. New alliances were underway.

"Oh, Mom, before you go, we were going to call you and Razor later. This morning we got our marriage license and would like to get married at Thanksgiving, just a private ceremony. Could we have a reception at your house? Whimsy Towers is better equipped than our place. I've already talked to Tim about coming, and he will try to get Elizabeth up for Thanksgiving. How's that for another raison d'être for gathering the family battalions?"

"Oh, Kev, that would be so wonderful!" I felt my eyes filling with tears. "Razor is right here, and I'll let him know the plans. This Thanksgiving without Dad and David will be a hard one, and I'm so glad for good news to be thankful for."

"Well, Massachusetts was the first state to legalize same-sex marriage, and we feel lucky to live here." Kev paused. "Mom, how are you doing? We do think about you a lot. Little Charlie is consuming our life, but you are in our thoughts. How difficult was it to return to Alexandria?"

"Thank you, Kev. It's been emotional, but Razor has been a huge help. I think I might have just stared at the walls for a few months without him. And he gives me energy. We can talk more later, but I'm making changes to improve my mental and physical health. I don't want you boys to worry about me, and there are things I can try to fix."

"We both love you, Mom, and tell Razor that Brad will call when he's free after feeding time—maybe about eighteen years!"

I hung up and let the tears come.

Razor could hear only my side of the conversation, and he stepped over and put his arms around me, not saying a word. Other than my occasionally taking his arm to steady me when we walked, Razor and I had never really touched since he took my hand at the funeral. I did not resist. I was glad for the comfort and for a brief moment of feeling safe.

"Sounds like some news," he said finally, relaxing his arms.

"Yes, their marriage is happening soon. I'm not sure anyone is invited to it, but they'd like a reception at Whimsy Towers. I hope you can plan to come for Thanksgiving and a wedding party. Or rather, *stay* for Thanksgiving and a wedding party!"

"I'd be so glad to. The only thing I plan in the fall is eating lots of oysters! I'm sorry to admit that my life is no longer very exciting. I enjoy the people and the volunteer work at the museum, but my time is flexible. Spending more of it on the Cape sounds like a good idea. I like reorganizing my priorities.

"I've never been driven by money and the accumulation of stuff. That's not my definition of success, which was at odds with my wife's. I made more money than we could ever spend, but it was not enough. These last few years have been a fresh beginning. And to see Brad's happiness is the best reward. His marriage and a child are terrific news. I wouldn't miss that party for anything."

I wondered what my definition of success might be. And did it change over time? How is a woman's definition different from a man's?

Razor pulled his hair back into a ponytail, making his dark eyes more prominent. He was dressed casually in blue jeans and red plaid shirt and was easily lifting the boxes we had organized and filled. I tried to picture him in his former life as James Bond: cocky, imperious, stiff tuxedo, beautiful women falling for him right and left. Razor was too low-key for my fanciful stereotype. He did not live for show and applause. He was an observer, a listener.

I wondered how the pursuit of success was linked to happiness and self-worth. I asked Razor how he would define "success" in life.

Without hesitating, he looked at me and answered, "Enduring love."

"That seems a high bar," I responded, feeling very inadequate—like a cautious observer of my own mismanaged life. Then I asked, "Is there someone you'd like to bring to Thanksgiving?"

"No, Theresa, there is no one," came the instant reply.

He resumed piling boxes in a neat row.

"Do you think your wife would want to come? Does she know about Kev?"

"My ex-wife, and I doubt it. I'll let Brad sort that out. I think he's pretty much written her off. She said some things that can't be unsaid." He stopped organizing boxes: "How can a mother turn her back on her child?"

I felt the weight of that question.

"Sometimes we speak what should not be spoken," I answered. "We don't give patience a chance. Our mouth gets ahead of our heart and can't get out of the way in time. Do you know the lines from 'The Rubaiyat of Omar Khayyam'?

> *The Moving Finger writes, and, having writ,*
> *Moves on; nor all your Piety nor Wit*
> *Shall lure it back to cancel half a Line,*
> *Nor all your Tears wash out a Word of it.*

"I don't mean to reduce your ex-wife's attitude to a quatrain of ancient poetry, but we cannot pull back our mistakes or retract reproach. We can, however, try to confront our reactions and learn from them. Does that sound preachy? Perhaps she's had time to reconsider what she is losing. It's not easy to be sorry, to be wrong. Might she soften or reconsider? Does she blame you?"

The last question brought a furrowed brow to Razor's face. He looked thoughtful and sad. "I think she blames me for everything that went wrong between us."

"Well, that's a heavy load," I responded.

"Divorce is defeat. There's no way around it. It's expectation gone awry. Her beautiful little boy traveled down a path she couldn't understand, and I supported him. She felt both of us had rejected her. Now she's lonely and angry. Bitter, really. We no longer speak. With a grown child, there's no particular need. I couldn't repair what seemed lost, and Brad was not interested in trying. Do you know the expression in a relationship of 'contribute or contaminate'? Our marriage contracted an illness that consumed it. We could not grow together."

I wanted to hug this kind man who was hurting. I thought of Kevin and was filled with regrets.

"Razor, I think in life we aim and miss at least as much as hitting the mark. Parenting is so complicated. I'm sure Brad's mother loves him. She's just not able to separate his hopes from hers."

"But isn't that the purpose of being a parent, of raising a complete and confident adult? Satisfying our own egos is not fuel for someone else's fire. She saw only her needs and not his. In a way, Brad became invisible to her when she could not accept his lifestyle, and something invisible cannot be touched or heard."

I thought back to my father needing to fulfill the roles of two parents. "I can remember when I was a teenager, girls were always talking about distancing themselves from their mothers, who they said just didn't understand them. Those years were a time of testing the boundaries of independence, of trying to outgrow parents. I yearned for the option of having a mother to reject."

"I'd say your father did a pretty good job." Razor was smiling, looking intently at me. "He must have really devoted himself to the assignment he was given. I'm sure it was not easy. Was it hard for him to see you set off on your own life?"

"Yes, it was. It was hard for both of us, but he wasn't in the business of holding me back. After college Kevin and I married, and we lived near my father for the rest of his life. I'm so glad we had that time together. He was my rock, my hero, but he couldn't open up parts of himself.

"He was not easily thrown off balance, but he struggled with carrying the weight of the past into the present. My father fought an internal battle with loss and life, missing my mother and wanting to be whole enough to raise me. I only learned of Whimsy Towers after his death."

"Do you think you'll spend more time there now?" Razor asked.

I was lost in thought and said aloud, "We cannot really know another person."

Chapter Seventeen

Cape Cod had put on its winter garment of somber gray. The last of the leaves had fallen, scattered on the ground like bits of cloth blown in fading red and yellow patterns on the grass. Razor dropped me at Whimsy Towers and continued on to Brad and Kev's. We had left Alexandria before dawn in order to arrive in the daylight, but it had been a long drive. Anxiety for destination is a strong motivator, and we were grandparents on a mission. They would all return the next day for dinner, and I could hardly wait to meet little Charles David.

My life was a pendulum, swinging from horror and grief to joy and optimism. I was alone with my Trojan horse, hiding what could burst forth. I tried to project a picture of normalcy, but there was ugliness lurking.

Perhaps I could shed the shell of regret and hypocrisy, relegating self-loathing to history. The temptation was to wrap my world tightly around me, but I wanted to be part of life's conversation.

New chapters bring fresh motivation and impetus. My grandson brings no personal ties to the past, but he carries the burden of drugs etched onto his clean slate. He is already a fighter. I will never hold him and feel apologetic and guilty. He is free of my mistakes. I'll ride the crest of this wave until I see Charles David as an untainted adult of his own making. Chances are I will not live to see it, but I can applaud his journey.

Mattie had warm lobster bisque still on the stove when I came in. The aroma drew me into the kitchen, and I stood and sipped huge spoonfuls right out of the pot. Whimsy Towers was where I felt the happiest, where I felt anchored. I did not long for Alexandria when I was in Cape Cod. I wondered how not having Kevin to come home to would change the balance of Virginia and Cape Cod. My life with Kevin was primarily in Alexandria, where we had raised our children. Razor's question about whether I'd be spending more time in Chatham was waiting for an answer to take shape.

In the few weeks I'd been gone, Mattie had returned to South Carolina and moved herself back to Whimsy Towers full time. She was now my resident support. My absent sons were glad, and I was glad of her company and her cooking. Mattie was easy to have around. She anticipated. She took control of schedules, ordering, and cleaning. The grass was cut, the fruit bowl always full, and a steady stream of biscuits found its way to Theodosia's tin bread box on the counter. Mattie liked responsibility.

What remained was for me to make changes, to introduce more positive behavior. I was determined to start and end the day with improving my mental and physical capacities. No more sliding through life.

I awoke to the sound of singing and slow, rhythmic clapping. It took a moment to rouse myself to awareness.

A new day was underway. I opened my bedroom door and could hear Mattie downstairs:

>*Roll Jordan, roll*
>*Roll Jordan, roll*
>*I wanter go to heav'n when I die*
>*To hear ol' Jordan roll*
>*O brethern*
>*Roll Jordan, roll*
>*Roll Jordan, roll*
>*I wanter go to heav'n when I die*
>*To hear ol' Jordan roll*
>
>*Oh, brothers you oughter been dere*
>*Yes my Lord*
>*A-sittin' in the Kingdom*
>*To hear ol' Jordan roll*

I grabbed my robe and made my way down the stairs. I couldn't help joining in the clapping as I entered the kitchen. Mattie turned and stopped when she heard me.

"Oh, I'm so sorry. Did I wake you?"

"No, no. I am sorry to have interrupted you. I love to hear you sing."

I knew that old spiritual was about the Israelites crossing the river to enter the Promised Land and had become a coded message for escape to American slaves. I teased Mattie: "Is there a reason you're celebrating laying down burdens and crossing to freedom this morning?"

I was glad when she laughed. Even painful connections to the past affirm our humanity. Mattie's ancestors had endured slavery, poverty, and injustice, but she had finished high school and already crossed barriers that would try to constrain her. *"Roll, Jordan, roll"* was the unstoppable power of the river, the force of freedom. A new life. Mattie had exceeded where others in her family had not. Alcohol was the current master that enslaved those she loved.

She sang an additional:

> *Roll Jordan, roll*
> *Roll Jordan, roll*
> *I wanter go to heav'n when I die*
> *To see ol' Jordan roll*

Mattie had an unstoppable belief in a wondrous afterlife. She believed that good behavior below was rewarded above. Heaven's door was open, ready for the tired and lost. Salvation followed suffering. I never asked her about other options.

"Oh no, no burdens. I'm feelin' today like the world is spilling out in generous helpings. I'm so happy to be lookin' out regular for you. I got extra gratitude. You've given me a safe home." She hesitated. "And you trust me."

"Mattie, I could not get along without you. Simple as that. We are a team around here."

She poured me some coffee, and I continued, "Tonight the whole Provincetown crowd is coming for dinner, three men and a baby. His name is Charles David. And then he and his grandfather will spend the night with us. Both parents must work tomorrow."

"It will be wonderful to have a baby around. I don't have children, but I'm hopin' they'll let me help."

"I'm sure those tired men will be grateful for all help!"

Mattie was quiet. "I've never told you, but I lost a baby when I was a teenager. Never even got to hold it. Seems long ago now."

"I'm so very sorry. What a terrible thing for you," I answered.

"Gets worse. It was my cousin who raped me. I was just fourteen. Nothin' came to him, and I've never been near a man since. Can't stand the thought of it, the violence."

"Oh, Mattie, not all men are sexual predators. Have you never met a man who was kind to you?"

"Oh, yes, but they stay kind to me from a distance. Not takin' any chances. I run fast as a scalded dog on wash day."

I thought of Theodosia's nurse housekeeper and the son she raised on her own at Whimsy Towers—a story that ended tragically with their deaths in a car accident the very first time they ventured to Boston.

"Well, Mattie, it's not too late. We'll just have to keep our eyes out for you! Though I don't like the thought of your leaving me."

I loved the richness of Mattie's language, a combination of her African and southern heritage. I wondered at her scalded dog simile and others such as "like a voice filled with smoke." Hints of her difficult life as a child being raised by relatives after her parents died came out in vignettes of speech: "I've never yet met a man whose character improved with drink" and "beware of poison wrapped in pretty packages." My favorite was, "Everybody that's talkin' 'bout Heaven ain't goin' there." Perhaps she was quoting another gospel song, but Mattie knew about making choices that matter.

She understood the value of community, of shared emotion. When David died, and I was trying to figure how many people might come to his funeral, Mattie said simply, "When somebody get sick, there be a crowd at that house, and there always be a crowd at grieving time."

I write for a living and am adamant about grammar and word usage. My poor sons didn't have a chance when they began a sentence with, "Me and my brother ..." or said, "I'm going to lay down" or "I'm feeling badly," but Mattie is a refreshing and honest addition to my life. And she is smart. I sometimes wonder how her life might have been different if she'd had educational opportunities and encouragement. She was stuck with the limits that came with her birth. No one who could have made a difference did.

Only a few years older than my sons, Mattie often observed conversations in silence and sometimes later tried out a new word. She was in between being an employee and being part of the family. One morning she said she was "beholden," with no reference. She was "smitten" by the avocado toast I made for myself and felt "injurious" that our weekly fresh produce delivery was late. Language is power, and Mattie was trying to find her way. She had access to a lifestyle different from the one she knew, but lacked the tools to navigate it.

She was building a new future brick by brick, and the foundation was going up slowly. Every generation—black, white, or brown—must redefine its purpose, its aspirations, within the confines of everyday demands. I was anxious to change direction, and Mattie was on her own course of improvement. Perhaps we could find some common ground.

"Mattie, I have an idea," I began. "I've received a postcard in the mail about some of the new classes being offered at the college for their next semester. There is one called 'Ireland and Irishness in Film,' and I'm thinking of taking it. What would you say to joining me? I'll pay."

"College?"

"Yes. It's community college. We could tackle it together. No need for worrying about grades but just to enjoy the information. Looks as though the class will watch movies there and also online, on our computers at home, and then discuss or maybe write about them. I could help you, and we could watch and talk about the movies together, before class. I think it sounds like fun. Will you try it?"

"Oh, my! My whole bones just gone limp. I can't see doin' college."

"Mattie, you are not seeing your potential. You graduated from high school, and I think you can do it. Give yourself a chance. There would be no pressure, and I know you like movies! Maybe it would be the beginning of a new road toward more education."

"A road to dead end! I be scared of that."

"Well, we don't have to register for awhile. Just think about it, okay?"

"I promise," came the answer that sounded as though it was lost in the dark, "but regular schoolin' barely sticks in my memory. It didn't come easy."

"All the more reason for an update! And also, Mattie, I'd like to get that white crib down from the attic. Do you think you can manage it, or shall we wait for reinforcements tonight? I want to have some things ready for Charles David. There's plenty of time before he's crawling around and making mischief, but I believe we still have some old baby gear that should work."

"I can do it, no problem, and I don't need to start dinner for distant time." Mattie hesitated. "Has Charles David been baptized?"

"I don't know. And I don't know if that's important to his parents."

She looked at me as though I had just told her that the sun would never shine again. Her eyes widened, and she blurted out, "But he's got to be baptized. He's an object of God's love and needs to be recognized."

I rather liked the idea of being recognized by a higher power, but I could not reassure her. "I'm afraid I have no say in the matter, and it's not so unusual these days to skip that ritual. I'm sorry to tell you that my own children were not baptized."

Mattie's jaw literally fell open. "Mr. David died without being baptized?"

I'd disrupted her world. She continued, earnestly, already knowing the answer to her question. "But he needs to find grace. He needs belongin' to God. I'll pray for him." She stopped and then became even more serious. "The devil looks for an opening and creeps in to collect. Tonight I'll put a broom across the door. Evil spirits want to come callin' and need to be stopped."

Mattie left the room. Her superstition remained.

Chapter Eighteen

Something palpable connected the almost-forty-year-old black woman and the tiny black baby she cradled in her arms. Charles David had arrived wrapped and cozy, calm and alert. His dark eyes followed the motion around him, and he stared into Mattie's eyes staring at him. I have never seen her looking so absorbed and happy. The baby fit easily against her body. I'm sure she was transported to a place of remembering that had deprived her of her own precious child, even if seeded by aggression and lust. A baby is warm innocence.

"He is so beautiful," she aloud to no one in particular. "He's a jumble of love, and we'll love him back." She looked up, "Mr. Kev and Mr. Brad, this baby is goin' to be a blessing."

"Thank you, Mattie. We are very excited to have him, though we hardly get enough sleep to re-charge ourselves. He's beginning to settle a little more, and they told us that holding him is the best medicine for withdrawal. It will take time."

Mattie took that instruction as a green light and began to sing to Charlie, holding him tight as she turned and walked away toward the kitchen.

"Well, there goes your child!" I said to my weary son. "Mattie will be your best helper. Obviously, I am not reliable on my own, but please know I would never take any chances with him by myself. Even without your father, we are a small team here to back you up. He is just adorable. I'm so very happy for you both."

Razor stepped forward and looked somewhat awkward, as if he wondered whether he should also kiss me after the boys did. He opted for no.

"What was the scene when you arrived late last night?" I asked him.

"Not like right now!" He laughed. "Charlie was testing his pipes and was keen not to allow any sleeping. The household was up long after I got there. I took a turn walking him, and I admit it brought back happy memories of Brad and those early days of being overwhelmed. This little guy has extra challenges, but he is tough and will come through. I'll tell you our two sons are amazing parents already."

Mattie was putting dinner together with one hand, not relinquishing the child content to be bobbed around close to her. It was normal for her to sing and work. We could hear her soft voice, soothing and melodious. She had set the table earlier in the day. The crib was ready with fresh sheets, and a swinging infant seat was in the dining room next to the table. Mattie liked organization, and she was not daunted by new chores.

The lobster bisque I had sampled before heading to bed was even better the next day. So many things in life seem to improve with patience and repetition. We sat down at the table, with no particular effort at placement.

ACT TWO

Theresa is seated next to Razor; Brad and Kev are across the table. The baby is swinging happily nearby. Candles flicker.

KEV: How nice to sit and have a peaceful meal served to us!

BRAD: I'm quite giddy at the prospect! We pretty much grab a bite on the go, in between changing and bathing and pacing with Charlie. Adult mealtimes have lost their regularity.

THERESA: How will you manage with work?

KEV: Well, we took some vacation time, but tomorrow is the first full shift. And thanks again for taking Charles David tonight. We both need to be at the restaurant for an important meeting in the morning but can stagger our workload after that. We also have an on-call woman who has fallen in love with our child.

Theresa laughs.

THERESA: Oh my, beware! Remember how Tim got sucked in by an older, attentive female!

KEV: Happily, she is a lot older than Elizabeth was and is married with her own two children. We can drop him off, and she has all the necessary equipment in a safe environment.

RAZOR: Speaking of safe environment, what is that hanging on Charlie's swing?

All eyes turn to the sleeping baby. Brad reaches over.

BRAD: It's a... it's a rabbit's foot. What in the world....?
THERESA: Oh, dear. Mattie, could you please come in?

Mattie enters with a pitcher of water to refill glasses.

THERESA: Mattie, I think maybe you've given Charlie a talisman for good luck?
MATTIE: A what?
THERESA: A charm. Something with magic power to fend off evil. A rabbit's foot?

Mattie looks down at the baby, avoiding eye contact with the adults.

THERESA: He is still an infant and not grabbing at anything, but you must know that we cannot have things within his reach that he could put into his mouth. It's really, really dangerous.
MATTIE: But I did it to keep him safe.
KEV: We understand that and thank you for your concern, but we hope you'll help us be vigilant, Mattie. Babies are too little to know what might choke them.
MATTIE: I'm sorry. I will try to be a vigilant.

All resume their soup, smiling. Mattie takes off the rabbit's foot and exits.

THERESA: Well, looks as though we are already losing our credibility as able caretakers at Whimsy Towers. I'm really sorry for that.

BRAD: She obviously meant no harm and has his interest at heart. I've even heard of dead chickens hung on the front door to ward off evil spirits.

THERESA: Please don't give her more ideas!

RAZOR: Theresa, I can come with Charlie when you are having him visit, if that would ease things. I've contacted the museum and told them I'm taking some time off to help here. I'd be glad to be another pair of eyes and hands for you.

THERESA: Thank you, Razor. You are coming to my rescue yet again, and I'm so grateful. We were a pretty good team in Virginia. And now Charlie's welfare is our first priority.

Razor stands and lifts his glass.

RAZOR: Let's drink to that. To Charlie! I serve with pleasure, Theresa, and tonight will be our maiden voyage. The boys will be glad to sleep through the night, if they can adjust their bodies to the luxury of it!

Everyone toasts. Razor sits down.

BRAD: I'm not sure I will sleep soundly again until he is off to college and on his own.

KEV: That sounds like a long way off! But it's true that part of me can no longer give in to deep sleep, like being perpetually on call and ready to respond when needed.

RAZOR: Trust me, he will not always want you to be light sleepers!

Laughter and low conversation as Mattie enters with a large platter of food.

BRAD: Smells wonderful, Mattie. Thank you so much.

KEV: And we are so glad that you will continue full-time with Mother. It really calms my mind to know that she's in such good hands. Thank you.

THERESA: I have a little plan that I'm trying to convince Mattie to join.

Eyes look toward Mattie, who is clearing away the soup plates.

THERESA: I've decided to enroll in a class at the community college on Irish film, and I want Mattie to join me. She's a little nervous about returning to school.

MATTIE: I be more than nervous.

KEV: What a great idea. I hope you'll accept the invitation, Mattie.

THERESA: For me, it's a necessary step to stretch my comfort zone. I've been out of college for half a century, but I want to test myself in new ways. I need greater mental exercise. My work is creative and wonderful, but I determine the timing on how it goes. I'm ready to be pushed a little, to have someone else set parameters for expanding my horizons. Frankly, I'm a little nervous, too.

KEV: Why not a graduate degree?

THERESA: That's a big commitment and too far to drive at the moment. And I don't want to settle for online classes. I want the challenge of real people in real time, with active voices that interact. Let's see how baby steps feel as I pick up the pace. Right now, I just need the prod close to home. I am serious about doing things that will increase my brain health, my mental capacity, and improve what feels like mental slipping. I think you will concur.

Time in a wheelchair was a wake-up call. A neurologist in the hospital got me seeing the possibilities. I've been reducing bread and sugar in my diet, eating more blueberries, fish, and avocadoes, and taking exercise more seriously. I want you boys to know that I'm on an earnest path of new beginnings and resolve. I do not want to be a burden or a problem to my children. Razor was my coach and steady companion in Virginia, and I so enjoyed it.

Celebrating the arrival of Charles David will forever coincide with my turning the page on my own new chapter. Kevin and I had only a peek at what might have been ahead for us as we moved through these retirement years together, but I am strengthened by the possibility that I can do this.

Eleanor Roosevelt said, "A woman is like a tea bag. You never know how strong she is until she's in hot water." Well, I have felt old age trying to overtake me, and I'm no longer willing to accept it. I come from a line of strong women who resist the status quo. No Goliath is too big for a determined woman with a pocketful of smooth stones ready to thrust at the enemy. Let the battle begin!

Theresa raises her glass toward the large portrait on the wall of her mother and grandmother. She is fighting tears.

And so ends the speech that I wanted you to hear tonight.

KEV: Bravo, Mother! We'll support you any way we can. Just let us know.

THERESA: Thank you, Kev. I don't mean to imply that this journey will be easy or short, but I have embarked on it and will not turn back. A fire in the belly must be tended, or it will die out.

KEV: Are we having carrot sticks for dessert?

THERESA: Close, but not quite. I'm not totally into depriving myself. We're having chocolate cake made from whole wheat and chickpea flour, bananas, carrots, beets, pineapple, zucchini, dates, currants, and three kinds of nuts. No sugar. It has a total of twenty-two ingredients and took Mattie about half a day to make!

The baby stirs and begins to make noise. Brad gives the swing a gentle push.

BRAD: I suppose that's our cue to eat and run.

RAZOR: We'll sleep with doors open, and I promise he will be fine. We might be a little rusty, but with three of us, Charlie will have lots of attention and care.

Mattie delivers individual pieces of cake.

BRAD: We're totally comfortable and appreciate how you've both welcomed our little stranger into the family. We feel so lucky. And yes, Mattie, we believe he is already a blessing.

KEV: But check back in sixteen years! Mom, this cake is delicious. Certainly not a sugar high, but an interesting mixture of flavors and texture. I can hardly get my head around a cake that has so many healthy ingredients. Well done!

THERESA: Thanks, Kev. My sweet tooth will live to see another day. Remember that we need to talk about your Thanksgiving party sometime. Tim called today and is definitely planning to bring Elizabeth. He will tie her to the mast for safe passage to keep her from drink this next week. I can't believe that in ten days we will all be together for the first time since losing David and Dad. And your party will be a welcome celebration. Just let me know when and what you need from me.

KEV: Brad and I look forward to it, too. Everything will be taken care of through the restaurant. We can't really stop this runaway Charlie train to catch our breath or cook, but our happy news might provide a break from grief.

BRAD: We'll see you a little later than this time to-morrow. Everything you need is in Charlie's bags. He's traveling with more luggage than most tourists, but we didn't want to risk not having something you'll need. Some of it we can leave here. Feel free to call with any questions—as if we have answers!

KEV: By the way, Mother, did you find any news about the family DNA testing in David's apartment?

THERESA: No, no revelations. I guess we are left with what we know. The ghosts can sleep.

Chapter Nineteen

"Theresa, you need to wake up! Wake up! We have a problem."

I tried to stir myself from my dream. I was picking apples with a man whose face was turned. We were barefoot in bathing suits, and the sun was hot. I thought it was Kevin, but then I heard Razor's voice somewhere, and I dropped my apples, pulled from the dream. A hand on my bare arm shook me awake.

"Theresa, please."

Razor was standing next to my bed, and sunshine filled the room.

"Charlie's gone! Wake up."

I bolted upright in my nest of pillows and soft covers. My nightgown slipped off my shoulder, and my tousled morning self faced Razor in full view of my pink satin top. "What? What are you talking about?" I asked, reaching for the sheet. Exposed skin is no longer seductive enticement or welcome viewing.

"What do you mean 'gone'?" I was slowly gathering my wits.

We had all been up several times in the night, feeding and comforting Charles David. We operated as baby triage, responding to his cries and changing his diaper, warming milk, and cajoling him back to sleep. It was a

LOVE & LIES | 179

long night, a vivid reminder of why people have children when they're young and resilient. Even healthy babies without drugs tormenting their bodies need time to settle into a waking/sleeping routine.

"He's not in his crib, and when I went downstairs, I expected to find him with Mattie, but she's not here either. There is fresh coffee but no sign of them. I've checked the house and everywhere outside. In the boathouse I found one of his booties." He held up a tiny, blue, hand-knit bootie. "Do you think she might have taken him?"

"Do you mean like kidnapping? Is my car here?" I asked, finally beginning to grasp the morning situation, after a disjointed night.

"Yes, it is."

"I cannot believe she would take him. I know she would never hurt him. She adores that little guy."

"Do you think we should call the boys?"

"No. No, not yet. There's nothing they could do. What time is it?"

"Eight-thirty," came the response. Razor was clearly concerned, but calm. His dark hair seemed more gray in the bright morning light, framing the worry on his face. Years in the CIA must have prepared him to approach emergencies with composure. He had gone through options and was ready for next steps. Razor was a man who did not react or presume. He analyzed. He stood for a moment, his flannel pajamas top loosely buttoned, and then sat down on the edge of the bed and leaned over, kissing me gently on the cheek. "We'll find them."

"I'll meet you downstairs in five minutes. There must be a reason," I said to the back of the tall man leaving my bedroom.

I dressed hurriedly, throwing on a heavy sweater and jeans that felt familiar and comfortable. A woman in her seventies does not look her best first thing in the morning. Bed hair and bad breath are daily reminders.

Mid-November was considered either late fall or early winter, and even sunny mornings were cold and unforgiving. The wind tried to unsteady us as we crossed the lawn toward the ocean. I shuddered to think of those before who had searched in vain for my mother and grandmother. The water churned in waves that rolled over large rocks next to the boathouse. The ocean held secrets and was a greedy neighbor.

We took turns calling Mattie's name, with no real expectation of being heard in the open, and the wind swallowed our sounds like a stifled echo. The beach was deserted. Even the seagulls stood still, bravely balancing on one leg and then the other. Occasionally, a sand crab or insect caught their attention and disrupted their stillness.

I held Razor's arm tightly as we made our way slowly in the dry sand. The houses closest to Whimsy Towers were now empty after the season, but we ventured off the beach toward each of them to check for Mattie and the baby. I kept hoping for a logical explanation, an answer that would not throw our world into chaos and add to the tragedies of my family. The ocean teased me with its power.

"Shall we admit defeat and call the boys?" I asked, not quite ready for the admission of failure.

"What's that?" answered Razor, squinting his eyes. "I saw something move across the beach. Way down there. See it?"

I couldn't see anything move, but my powers of observation were not on a par with Razor's. His step quickened, and I was surprised that I could keep up with him, still holding his arm. We moved in rhythm, like horses yoked together.

"There! There's a person. Can you see?"

I felt like a silent partner, unable to contribute.

"Theresa, I'm going to run ahead. Are you all right following on your own?"

"Yes, I think so."

"Just take it easy. I don't want to lose a lead."

And off jogged Razor, with a determined stride and focus straight ahead. I watched him shrink in my view, until he was a colored blur far down the beach. I moved closer to the water, where the sand was damp and firmer for walking alone. Had Razor's instincts brought his talents to bear? I felt oddly comforted that somehow his professional training had begun to unravel our mystery.

It took me a long while to walk the distance down the beach, and there was no sign of Razor. I kept expecting him to come into my sight. I don't believe I had ever been so far down on the beach. When I was first at Whimsy Towers, my dog Gypsy was no longer able to walk very far, and we were often enticed into the water, to be carried along by summer waves. Legs that struggle on land are encouraged in water.

I needed to sit down. Surely one of the houses had left heavy Adirondack chairs out for the winter on their lawn. Walkers beyond their limits need rest. I was out of breath as I turned up a slight incline through tall grasses toward a house and tried to keep my balance in the deeper sand.

I fell, landing in a clump of soft grass.

"Theresa!"

In an instant, several sets of arms were lifting me up. White hands and black hands. As I steadied myself between two men, Razor was still holding on to me. He said, "I was just about to come back down the beach for you. Theresa, this is Joseph Burns."

Mattie stood nearby, holding a sleeping Charles David, who was bundled up in a coat, hat, and warm blanket.

"Hello, Joseph. I apologize for my entrance. I need a lesson on balance from those seagulls!"

"How do you do, ma'am. We were watching for you but didn't expect you to cut up that little hill. Are you all right?"

"Oh yes, thank you, but 'all right' is relative these days."

Razor looked down at me and smiled.

"Please come inside and have something warm to drink," Joseph continued. "I've been sitting in the folly with Mattie and Charlie, but she wouldn't come into the house. I'd like to offer you some refreshment."

Joseph pointed to a whimsical and decorative structure in the shape of an octagon, with open sides, as we walked toward the main house. It could not have been more than twelve feet wide. The folly had columns and illogical windows, with winter-empty flower boxes. A weather vane in the shape of a sailboat topped the pointed slate roof.

"It's warm there in the sunshine and actually nice in all seasons. Like a playhouse for grown-ups."

Joseph took us through the unlocked door of a massive, three-story house. It was the biggest house I had seen in Chatham, on the ocean or not. It had simple lines, of wood construction, with unimposing architectural detail that primarily consisted of dark shutters held open by black shutter dogs shaped like bunches of grapes. This house did not make a flashy statement of its owner's wealth with gaudy gates and high walls with security cameras and warning signs. It spoke of old Cape Cod, of family gatherings to share vacations of touch football on the lawn, croquet, strawberry scones with lemonade, and stiff drinks served under umbrellas at dusk. It whispered welcome. I wondered whether Theodosia had known the owners here in her day.

"What a beautiful home!" I exclaimed as we stood in a large hall lined with paintings of sailboats straining under sail and sailboat races on sunny days. An old oil painting with gilded frame of a square-rigged ship in choppy waters held place of honor in a prominent position between two doors. Next to it was a tall brass binnacle with polished wooden base, standing guard, ready to chart a course. Low tables held photographs of smiling men on boats, holding trophies, wearing white. White men.

"Thank you," replied Joseph, "but I am just the caretaker here. The owners live in New York. I've been with them for many years, serving in the city and here on the Cape. I confess I love it here, even when the quiet of winter settles over all the bustle of parties in season, leaving just the sounds and fragrance of nature."

"I think you are a poet, Joseph!" I replied. His dark face flushed.

"I was outside, picking up debris from the storm last night, when I saw Mattie standing at the water's edge. She didn't look distressed or in trouble, but it's cold and windy out there, and I saw she was carrying a baby. I went and asked if she'd like to sit awhile, and we've been in the folly for an hour or more, talking."

He looked at Mattie with a sheepish grin, and she hugged the baby tighter.

"I hope I didn't worry you," she began. "Charlie woke up fussy, and I didn't want him to wake you again. We'd already had quite a night! I took him down to the boathouse, but he wouldn't settle, so I started to walk. He loves walkin'. This little precious loves walkin' and lovin'."

"And who wouldn't?" said Joseph, still wearing a grin aimed at Mattie.

Razor picked up the story. "Joseph was chasing Mattie's hat that the wind had snatched at the folly and blown across the beach toward the water. That's what I saw in the distance. Hats off to a hat—the clue that broke the case! We were at the point of giving up and turning back."

Joseph led us into the kitchen, where we could smell coffee and baking. "Believe it or not, I made cinnamon buns this morning. No particular reason; I just like to bake. Shall we have some? I'm so glad for the company."

Razor and I looked at each other, smiling, as we took off our coats. Mattie handed me Charles David and began to help Joseph with plates and serving. He poured coffee into mugs that had pictures of different birds on them, and we sat at a round table in a sunny kitchen, like two couples plucked from a fairy tale.

"How long have you lived here?" Joseph asked, looking not quite sure whom he should be addressing. "Have you always been local?"

"Yes, and no," Razor began. "We are a family in flux, a mixture, but we're all so happy here on the Cape." He continued with the relationship of our sons, Mattie taking care of me, and his desire to be more involved with the family. "Theresa's grandmother bought Whimsy Towers, and now her great, great-grandson has arrived on the scene."

We all looked at Charles David, who was beginning to stretch and reach out tiny hands from under his blanket. Little fists made their way to his open mouth, his head turning in response to our voices. Mattie excused herself to warm a bottle for the waking baby. She moved around the kitchen as if she knew her way.

"She is so good with him," Joseph said. He watched her moving comfortably in his domain. "She's a kind woman," he said to no one in particular.

"So will you stay here all winter?" I asked, breaking Joseph's gaze at Mattie.

"I'm not sure. Sometimes there is a big New Year's Eve party at the house. We light all the fires, and every room is still decorated with trees, garlands, sparkling ornaments, and greenery. Many guests arrive by private plane or helicopter on the front lawn. Even a small orchestra is flown in from New York. It's a wonderful party, but most events are less formal these days." He sighed. "Changing times and busy schedules." Then he laughed to himself. "I'm the old shoe. I go where I'm needed, but the other staff stay with the owners, especially now that the children have scattered. New generations have different tastes and live farther away, and it's harder and harder to get them to spend time in Chatham. Fourteen empty bedrooms is a lot of unused real estate!"

We all laughed. "Goodness," I said, "that makes my situation a lot more workable!"

"Do you have children, Joseph?" Razor asked.

"No, I never married, though I know that's not a requirement. Being in service has kept me occupied, especially when I traveled a lot with the family, but I do care for a nephew who's been in some trouble and needs my help. He's almost eighteen now. Some young men seem to struggle with finding their way and avoiding a path of dead-end darkness, but it's hard not to get swept up in someone else's possibilities when you see them. He wants the end before the beginning. He's handsome and smart but thinks football and celebrity are the road to riches. His high school football performance has been impressive in a small town but will not dazzle professionals.

"Funny thing is, he's wonderful with animals. He senses their temperament, and they just seem to trust him. He's really gentle with helpless creatures. He'd be an amazing veterinarian, and I've offered to send him to school, but he's fighting his own nature. Like other young men I've known, he only wants lots of money and beautiful women on each arm." Joseph paused, looking earnest and wistful. "It's a tenacious stereotype and will end up wasting his talents and stealing his future."

"Theresa and I both have sons, older sons now, but peer pressure and uncertainty of choices are hard at that age. He's lucky to have your interest in him."

"Thanks, but the check-writing uncle is fast losing patience. I've just turned forty, and I need to plan for my own future, as well. Sometimes it gets a little lonely and isolated here these days, and I need to think ahead. Stay tuned."

Joseph smiled and sipped his coffee.

We sat in silence for a moment, and I noticed Mattie, head bowed, softly repeating the words "tenacious stereotype," as she fed Charles David his bottle.

Chapter Twenty

"I hope Charlie wasn't too much trouble," Kev began. "Brad and I had a great night's sleep, and I actually felt a little guilty."

"Then we got over it!" continued Brad, laughing. "Was everything all right?"

"Oh, yes, no problem," answered Razor, avoiding eye contact with me. "Charles David reminded us, repeatedly, that children shake up our lives! What we think is routine is suddenly obsolete. But we had a great time with him and are so glad we could be here for you. We all worked really well together, and Mattie was especially helpful. She was our champion and has more energy than we might have found on our own. She has built-in batteries that don't seem to need charging as often as ours!"

I could hear Mattie singing in the kitchen. It was not her usual gospel melody or rhythm. It sounded like hip hop—terse, tight syllables punctuated by gasping consonants in a row. As I came up behind her at the sink, I heard something about a "*scrub*" and "*no love.*" The song had a lyrical cadence, like poetry in short bursts.

When Razor came in and approached me, Mattie heard us and turned. "Oh, sorry. I get a little too enthusiastic sometimes, too carried away. I was havin' a talk with myself."

"What's that song about?" I asked.

"It's from my growin' up days. Very popular when I was half this age, almost twenty years ago. Called 'No Scrubs,' by a sassy girl group, TLC."

"I've never heard you sing that kind of music before," I replied, genuinely curious. "Are you a secret rapper?"

Mattie looked down. "My family didn't approve anything outside the church music, but young people always be interested in the message that fits them."

"What's a 'scrub'?"

"Loser men are scrubs, or 'busters,' hanging out car windows callin' at women. Disrespectful. They mostly what I knew."

Razor began to smile. "Is there a reason this subject comes to mind today?" He looked at me, and I understood his meaning. "Perhaps related to the events of our morning on the beach?"

Mattie hesitated. We had no right to inquire into her personal feelings, but we had been witness to her meeting an interesting and thoughtful man about her age, and we were both impressed with him.

"Mattie, we don't mean to pry," I added, kidding myself. "We really liked meeting Joseph, but I know you are not eager to encourage a man."

Kev and Brad came into the kitchen to make cappuccinos and asked if we'd like one.

"Absolutely, if you have time to stay, but decaf for me, please. Razor?"

"Yes, thanks. Decaf and a good night's sleep!"

Mattie had not moved from the sink. She stared out the window. "He assumed Charlie was my baby." And still not looking at anyone, she continued, "I almost wanted to lie, to claim that beautiful black child as my own. I felt his needing me, dependin' on me, and I wanted to be the one who cared for him. I wanted to feel important. A few minutes of havin' my own family, with a nice man and a baby."

Brad and Kev had walked into an odd conversation and looked a little puzzled. I felt we needed to explain the minimum necessary.

I began, "We were walking far down the beach this morning, farther than I'd ever been in that direction, and Mattie was carrying Charles David. He was happily bundled up, and the sun was warm. By accident, we met a caretaker for one of the houses. He invited us in for coffee, and we enjoyed a wonderful visit."

Mattie resumed, "Can you picture Joseph bein' a scrub? There was gentleness in him."

"Yes, there was," replied Razor. "He is a man with a giving nature. I doubt he would ever disrespect a woman, or anyone. And I think he rather fancied you, Mattie. Don't slam a door that hasn't even quite opened. Would you be willing to see him again?"

"Please say 'yes,' Mattie. You know you could invite him here anytime, if you didn't want to go out in public somewhere. This is now your home, too," I added.

"Our son is clearly more popular than we are," said Kev. He and Brad laughed. "He's like a magnet wherever he goes. And maybe now he's a matchmaker!"

We all joined in the laughter, and little Charlie cooed at his doting parents. Mattie took the baby from Kev's arms, saying, "You little thing are just too cute!" and promptly handed him back. Kev easily cradled his wide-awake son in one arm and reached for Brad's hand. I felt their journey into parenthood was on solid ground.

"Mother, we're making plans for our party the Saturday after Thanksgiving, if that's all right with you. We thought a luncheon might be better this time of year. We can roll out the awning and use the patio for serving and maybe some music. The space heaters should keep the chill off. The restaurant will handle everything, and we'll send out invitations tomorrow."

"That would be perfect, Kev. I'm hiring some help for Mattie for Thanksgiving dinner, and they can leave things however you'd like. Susan and her parents will be coming, but it will feel very different this year. I really want to focus on gratitude and not loss."

"And on that topic of gratitude, we have some news. Brad and I have an appointment to get married on Wednesday at 2:00 o'clock. We'd like you and Razor to be there. A simple ceremony at the Registrar's office. With luck, Charles David will be a sleeping participant! Tim was sworn to secrecy while we coordinated the details with work, but he and Elizabeth are coming in the day before, so that they're sure to be here. It means a lot to us to have just our family together. Friends can celebrate at the party Saturday."

"How fantastic!" exclaimed Razor, stepping over to hug his son. "A party for a new baby and a new beginning together. Congratulations!"

"Absolutely," I added, and then broke into tears.

Kev handed the baby to Brad and came to put his arms around me. "Mom, it's all right. I know you have a lot to handle. This Thanksgiving will not be easy for you, or for Tim and me. Or Susan, either. We share those empty spaces that remind us of past happiness, but those spaces will gradually fill with new joy and happiness. Grief cannot become a lifestyle. Nobody sinking in quicksand wants their loved ones to jump in to help them. We need lifting out, and Dad and David would be the first to offer a hand."

"You're right, Kev, and thank you for being here with your marvelous good news."

I felt unworthy of happiness. Had I caused the death of my son?

I tried to stop crying but could not, reminding myself of death and deceit. I was Janus-faced, like the mythological Roman god Janus who was guardian of doorways and passages, patron of beginnings and endings. He is depicted as having two faces, one in the front and the other at the back of his head, looking to both the future and the past. He represented the duality of life lived in two directions.

I was his two-faced descendant, living two versions of a life. One face kept rehearsing the accident that killed my child, and the other face celebrated the wonder of life—an innocent baby, good friends, and the future.

Kev continued to hold me tight, letting my tears have their time, like unstoppable messengers of sorrow.

"Well, we need to get on home and ready ourselves for what the night will bring," said Brad. "Charles David is so quiet and full of smiles until the house is dark and still. Then he seems to need company to comfort him, perhaps to reassure him that the darkness will not last."

"Thanks again for all the help," added Kev, releasing me. "We're lucky to have you so close. Well, an hour is not exactly close, but better than Virginia or Maryland." He paused. "Razor, what's your plan? Are you coming or staying?"

"Well, I ...."

"Oh, please do stay," I interrupted. "We can finish our coffee and have a quiet night."

"I accept. Maybe I can help around here to get ready for Thanksgiving."

We said good night, with kisses all around, and Mattie hugged Charlie's blanket before she draped it over the smiling baby that watched her with big, brown eyes.

She finished in the kitchen, and Razor and I settled onto the couch.

"Tell me why you come here, Theresa," Razor asked.

"That sounds like a loaded question!"

"Not loaded, just penetrating, I hope. I'm really curious."

"Well, first I came because I inherited Whimsy Towers and had known nothing about it. It was a missing piece of my family history, a piece I didn't even know was missing. I came that first summer to think about my life, my marriage, my future. It was certainly an escape."

"And you chose not to stay, to run away permanently?"

"Yes, I chose commitment. With Timmy on the way that fall and a husband who had done nothing wrong, I felt I needed to make some adjustments about my expectations in life. I had felt suffocated but didn't know how to get free, but free isn't always the answer. For us, communication was the answer."

"And Kevin agreed?"

"Kevin wanted our marriage to work and was willing to try. I admit we both struggled. I was the hothead, and he was the unflappable one. We finally had to meet somewhere in the middle, and we reshaped our life by what we expected from it. I think we do not really see the world as it is; we interpret it only through our own lens."

"I envy you," Razor said after a moment. "My wife and I were not so clear-headed."

"It's odd now to think back on the challenges of that time. Hopes, fears, and disappointments fell into categories, to be poked and evaluated separately, but really it's a seamless garment. Without sounding too philosophical, life is a collage of changing relationships and attitudes that disrupt what seems fixed."

"'Fixed' is the stumbling block," replied Razor, smiling with the expression of a man who had figured out his way and was at ease. He took a sip of coffee and put his cup on the side table. "When we can't shake loose our old patterns and prejudices, we can't move forward. 'Stuck' is not progress."

"Kevin and I eventually found our comfort zone." I paused and sighed, looking into the eyes of a man sitting a little too close to me on the couch. "I can't imagine a disagreement with you rising to a point out of reach. I can't picture you in an argument. Razor, may I be so bold as to say that you seem easy to live with, to be around?"

"May I be so bold as to kiss you?"

He did not wait for an answer, and I did not resist. His arms were strong as he pulled me toward him, and we leaned back into the cushions.

Chapter Twenty-One

My first night with Razor was a reawakening. I felt the stirrings of passion as we kissed on the couch and soon found our way to my bedroom. I felt nimble in the hands of a man who caressed my body and covered me with gentle, yet hungry, kisses. Fear of nakedness disappeared. Reluctance about sexual intimacy was vanquished. My widow's cruse filled with desire and overflowed. I was alive in his arms and eager for him.

"This is crazy," I whispered, ignoring the obvious signals that repeated a call to stop: too soon, too old, too soon, too old....

"Let me love you," was the simple answer.

Razor and I rolled to the edges of the bed, gasping for breath and melting into lovemaking that didn't distinguish age or propriety. Theodosia's bed resumed its role of welcoming star-crossed lovers that defied the rightness of behavior. I could not have planned such conduct or imagined sharing my bed with another man after Kevin's death. I did not think I was looking for intimacy. I did not think my soft, reluctant body could want it.

Razor was agile and athletic, but not aggressive. He easily lifted me into greater pleasure, and I soared at his touch.

We finally lay back on mounds of pillows, with just a crumpled sheet for cover.

"Theresa, I was attracted to you the day we met, at David's funeral."

I laughed and smoothed back his long hair. He had seen something in me that lay in wait. "An incapacitated, married woman, wrapped in bandages—now there's a vision of attraction!"

"I think I've just proved I could lift you out of a wheelchair and into my arms—and into my life." He mockingly turned and lifted me up onto him, kissing me and reigniting desire.

"I've tried to be the perfect gentleman, perfectly smitten but anxious to be respectful and patient. Being with you those weeks in Alexandria was a mighty struggle. You can't imagine how much I wanted to kiss and hold you, to comfort you. We sat in front of the fire and connected without anything physical happening between us, but my mind raced to the possibilities."

"Razor, shall we face the obvious?" I remained on top of him and looked hard into his eyes. "This is crazy, which I believe is the first thing I said when we fell into my bed. It is wonderful and crazy, but I'm too old for you. And spent."

He smiled a naughty smile, and I felt his gentle, scratchy hand moving slowly across my leg. "Not too old. Not too old for genuine feelings. And definitely not spent! This is not some momentary fling, Theresa; I want to be by your side."

"Razor, I was already in high school when you were born!"

"Well, I'm glad you waited for me. It just took awhile to catch up. And how much older did you tell me your grandmother was than Stormy?"

He had won the argument with one sentence.

I surrendered with a long kiss and his firm, warm body holding me close.

Sleep came easily.

⅓

A knock on the door was followed immediately by Mattie entering with a cheerful "Good morning." She carried a tray but stopped in her tracks when she saw Razor in my bed. "Oh! Oh, I'm so sorry. I didn't realize.... I saw the empty bedroom and assumed you'd...." She put down the tray and stammered, "I'll bring another cup."

Razor and I could not help but laugh. We did not have time to respond before Mattie had hurriedly left the room. I was sorry to have embarrassed her, and I'm sure she was shocked, but it was not routine for her to bring me coffee in bed.

Razor kissed me tenderly on the cheek, his soft lips like the flutter of a butterfly deciding where to land for nectar.

"I'm no longer used to waking up with a man—especially a man who doesn't belong here!"

"I'd like to belong here, Theresa. Can we work on it?"

"Can I have an hour in the bathroom every day before you look at me?"

He pulled me into him and whispered, "I like the morning you just as much."

"As much as what—an old woman whose life has crashed, who is unpredictable in mind and body?"

"No, as much as the smart, witty, and beautiful woman I finally got to kiss last night."

"A little more than kissed! Razor, you are delusional. And I feel disloyal and a little embarrassed."

I didn't, however, move away from him.

"You are not disloyal, Theresa. You had a good marriage and a good husband, but Kevin is gone. Please don't pass on a chance to be happy again."

"This is just so soon, too soon. You've caught me off guard, and I feel guilty...."

The bedroom door was still open, and Mattie entered with hot biscuits and another cup for coffee. She did not offer to pour.

"Thank you, Mattie. I think you'll be seeing more of Mr. Razor at Whimsy Towers."

She did not answer, but left the room smiling.

"Just give it time, Theresa. Take your time, but tell me that we can explore this together. We're already coordinating on day care responsibilities for Charlie, and I'm a good anchor for you."

"Do you mean for the unstable and dissolute widow?"

Razor gathered me tight in his arms, and our two naked bodies were in no hurry for coffee.

I felt like a younger version of myself. My arms and legs wrapped easily around this man who warmed my bed and who looked at me with eyes that seemed to see beyond wrinkles and age. It was strange to feel desired and desirable.

Finally I asked, "Razor, what do you really want?"

"I want to wake up every day in this bed. I want to be the one you look to for support and encouragement. I want to be a strong arm and a ready listener. Theresa, you are amazing. You deserve to be happy. Deserve a fresh start. I know it's early after Kevin's passing, but I think we are good together, and I'd like to be there for you. In a curious way, I think Kevin would be glad. I know this is not what you were looking for or perhaps even wanting again, but I believe we can have something special, something good. Intimacy is more than sex."

"But quite a delicious by-product," I answered, a bit too quickly, as I settled back into his arms. I was surprised how my whole body had reacted and wanted him. What I thought was long dead had resurrected—like my dormant daffodil bulbs that lay unobserved in the ground, until the heat of the springtime sun brought forth their beauty and vitality. Razor was my stimulus. His optimism gave me the taste for more—more intimacy, more time with an interesting and handsome man, and more sex.

"Razor, I've led a complicated life. I have secrets and regrets."

"We all have secrets and regrets, Theresa. Being vulnerable and open in a relationship does not mean

exposure of our rawest elements. We do not turn ourselves inside out for another person but share what rises
to that level of caring that connects us."

"I'd like a relationship like that."

"Inshallah," he responded, kissing my forehead.

"What does that mean?"

"It's a frequent and beloved expression in Arabic. It
means 'God willing.'"

慓

We did not readily leave the ruffled bed to face a day
of duties. Razor explored the curve of my back, as I lay
on my stomach and welcomed his touch. I was trying to
foresee a future with this muscular, younger man who
was pleading his case. He brought vigor and determination to my bed and my life. Could I restart old longings?
There was no longer infidelity related to my temptation.
A dead husband cannot be deceived.

"Razor, do you play tennis?" I asked.

"Yes, but not in awhile. My ex-wife and I played dou-
bles at the club. Why?"

"I'd like to take lessons in the spring. I'd like to be
here in Chatham."

"Do you mean not going back to Virginia?"

"No, I think winter in Alexandria is still right, but I'd
like to be at Whimsy Towers when the weather breaks.
I've never seen it recovering from snow and cold."

"And where would you like me to be?"

I rolled over and let him slide over me like a wave. His hair fell around his face, tickling my shoulders. As he slowly arched his body, lifting me up and pushing a pillow under us, I forgot the question.

The tall case clock downstairs chimed eleven times. We were already lost in the moment and didn't need reminders.

As Razor finally pulled away, I felt his heart pounding. After a few minutes of reorganizing the bed, he flashed a broad grin. "That clock is like a watchman on patrol, urging a reveille to begin the day, before afternoon overtakes the morning."

"I think the day has begun in a most wonderful way," I responded and drew him back, throwing my arms straight out sideways on the bed like a splayed sacrifice under the weight of my new lover. "The clock is just a reminder of time slipping away. You've been very persuasive in encouraging me to pay attention."

Razor leaned over and began kissing my extended arms.

"Is that a 'yes' to letting me unpack my suitcase? I'll throw in teaching you to play tennis!" He laughed, and I knew I could not refuse him, or wanted to.

"How do we explain this to our children?" I asked. "Sneaking about usually goes the other way 'round."

"I think we should just say that I'll be spending time here, giving Kev and Brad space, and helping you get stronger, going on walks, playing Scrabble and mind-challenging games."

"And other physical strengthening of a more intimate nature?"

He continued to smile at me but was perfectly serious. "Yes, Theresa, I want to make love to you with hardly taking a breath, but I want us to share a life, to depend on and trust each other. Difference in age is only an excuse for not trying. I think we've established compatibility and a track record of enjoying each other's company and conversation—as well as a connection that makes sparks fly." He slid his hands under me. "We got a good start in Alexandria. A sensible start. Let's give it a chance to see where it takes us."

"I'm in," I said simply. "I don't want to see you go."

With no further prompting, my body succumbed again to forgotten sensations. Razor was reminding me of the possibilities of anxious desire, feelings that had not surfaced in many years. I was hesitant about keeping up with a man so full of plans and energy, but I wanted to conquer my apprehension and my fear that he had arrived too late.

"Let's drive to Provincetown and have lunch at The Lobster Pot," I suggested, out of breath, "or this day is going to pass us by."

"Sounds perfect. We can test our poker faces, if our boys are working. And I can pick up my things."

"Razor, I'd like us to maintain two bedrooms, to sleep together but not broadcast it. Not yet."

"Do the hall floors squeak?" he asked mischievously, kissing me into silence. "We've already crossed the bridge to Mattie's imagination."

We both laughed and headed to a hot shower of soapy pleasure. Whimsy Towers had a memory for new beginnings.

I did not want to risk losing what I had yet fully to experience. Living with Mattie was a good solution to my situation, but including Razor offered new direction—and unexpected benefits. He swept in like a fierce wind that would not change course. Could I empty my bucket of blame, guilt, and remorse to fill it with hope and rapture, to be with a man who wanted in my life? Could hating myself make room for loving another? Could I be free of guilt?

My cane seemed an odd necessity after a night of lovemaking. Physical activity in bed did not require balancing on two feet. Now my *mental* imbalance was even more in question: What was I thinking? The light of day only broadcast my physical deficiencies of age, but Razor made no mention of them. Flabby arms and legs with veins that looked like road maps were part of the skin I was wrapped in.

Razor put a large towel around me, and we resisted the urge to add another memory to the morning. The once-young body of an ice skater still wanted to excel and triumph; I wanted more. He rubbed my hair, and I took the towel and dropped it on the floor.

"How late do they serve lunch?" I asked.

"We'll be looking at dinner, at this rate," he answered, laughing, as he picked up the towel and hung it on the bar. "Come on, we have an honesty test to take."

I shuddered at the word. Dishonesty led to lies, and I was a master of both. Perhaps our sons would sense our false story. And then I wondered why it mattered.

"Mattie, I'm sorry for no notice, but we are going out for lunch today," I said, as we brought the tray back into the kitchen.

"I thought not to start anything," she answered. "But what about dinner?"

"Yes, we're definitely here for dinner," Razor answered, and added, "Mattie, I'm going to be here for awhile. I don't want to add extra work for you, and I hope I can do some things around here, too. I'm a pretty good cook, if you'll let me help. I think we already all work well together as a team. Does that sound all right?"

"Yes, sir, I welcome you bein' here. It's too tempting for her to fall into sadness."

The drive to Provincetown was predictable and uneventful. We chatted about our sons and their childhoods, the difficulty of knowing when to stop protecting them from the world, and how easy it was to fall off track in parenting. Razor often reached over and touched my leg, leaving it warm in place or patting gently. He was naturally affectionate, and I craved the attention.

The streets in downtown Provincetown were empty, and parking was not a problem in the off-season. Before long, the town would close up for winter, leaving residents to find entertainment and pleasure behind closed

206 | ANN HYMES

doors. Kev and Brad could both be full-time parents for a few months. I held Razor's arm and didn't bring my cane as we walked a short distance into the restaurant. The aroma immediately reminded me that we had skipped a proper meal that morning.

As we passed the cooking station, Brad saw us and called out, "Hey, strangers, what have you been up to?"

We looked at each other and probably blushed crimson.

Brad came out and escorted us to a table at the window. "You look like guilty teenagers," he said, staring at his father. "Did you sleep till noon after your previous night of baby duty?"

Razor mumbled something about catching up on sleep before he changed the subject and asked Brad about the specials for the day. I had just witnessed this ex-CIA operative navigate his way through an amorous minefield, unscathed.

"We are starving," I began, "and we have some news."

Razor looked at me and then at his son, who began to smile.

"Okay, never mind, I'm just going to put it out there. Your father and I slept together. And we liked it and are going to continue. No grand plans or expectations, but he is going to stay at Whimsy Towers."

"Well, that's a new chapter, Dad. Bravo!"

Brad bent over and kissed me on both cheeks. Razor looked stunned, as though I had just revealed his credit card number to everyone in the restaurant.

"And may I call you Mom?" Brad asked, teasing.

"You may not!"

"So much for subtlety and subterfuge," said Razor, reaching for my hand across the table. "We weren't sure we could pull it off, anyway."

"I've maxed out on secrets," I continued. "Caring about someone should not stay in the shadows."

"Sorry, but I need to call Kev. I hope he's not snoozing with the little prince. He won't want to miss this."

Brad left us, and Razor looked at me in disbelief. "Are you sure?"

"The cat has rather left the bag," I responded, "and I don't want to feel guilty about what is happening between us. It is soon, I admit, after losing Kevin, but it's honest and wonderful. You are waking me up to myself."

"Theresa," began Razor, "do you want me to fall in love with you? You are setting me on that course, you know."

"It's a zigzag course and loaded with potholes!" I answered. We both laughed, but I was serious.

We shared Russian Oysters, with sour cream and caviar, and then we each had blackened tuna. Our tastes mingled easily. We ordered two Mochaccinos for dessert, the Ghirardelli chocolate adding to a sweetened morning of heightened surprise.

"I love this day," I said matter-of-factly, as Kev walked into the restaurant holding Charles David.

"What's this news?" he blurted out, coming straight to the table and handing the baby to me. He shook Razor's hand and said, "This is great! I am so happy to hear it. Did you wake up in an alternative universe?"

"Truth is, we woke up in the same universe, in the same bed." I paused, looking down at the sleeping baby. "Kev, I know it sounds a little surprising, a little beyond unexpected, but I hope you're not too shocked or displeased with me. It's not a betrayal of your father. Neither of us saw this coming."

"I saw it coming!" said Razor quickly. "I saw it and wanted it, but my good breeding kept me from pouncing. I have learned patience in my line of work. Your mother is worth waiting for."

Kev hugged and kissed me, waking the baby in my lap. "Yes, she is. I think it's wonderful, Mother, just wonderful. I'm so glad for you both."

Charlie's screams signaled the end of lunch, and we left together, three generations of a family finding its way.

Chapter Twenty-Two

"And now how do we proceed, captain?" I asked Razor after we'd picked up his things and were headed back to Chatham.

"One day at a time. First, I'll return to St. Michaels and make some arrangements. Maybe after Thanksgiving and the party. I'd like to continue to rent my house in town and let the maritime museum use it for interns and visiting speakers. I'll check with my landlord, but I don't think she'll mind. And maybe I can entice you there for a weekend occasionally, when it's available. St. Michaels is not that far from Alexandria, and it's pretty nice in all seasons. I'd like you to see more of the work we've been doing."

"I'm afraid you are now officially, and publicly, stuck with me."

"I love the sound of that," he replied, nearly veering off the road.

"Will you miss the boat building?" I asked, rubbing his rough hand in mine and remembering it moving across my bare body. "You are making a big change, a leap of faith."

"Actually, I've been thinking about that, even before I dared to hope you would be more than a fellow grandparent. There are terrific programs that draw young men from the courts who've been in trouble and might have an interest in boat building. Or even just like working with their hands. These young men, and a few women, need structure and confidence, but they mostly need a second chance. Judges have seen the value in mentoring and learning marketable skills. Some young men have even come out of prison into these programs. Alexandria has a really good one: The Alexandria Seaport Foundation. They operate right in Old Town on the Potomac River. I was thinking that I could get involved with something like that on the Cape by learning in Alexandria."

He looked at me for a reaction. "And I promise I would be more attentive about wearing gloves."

"Razor, is there anything about you not to like?"

He pulled the car over onto the sandy shoulder and leaned toward me. "I am far from perfect. Theresa, we all grow into imperfect people, but each day begins afresh. I can be impatient when I see possibilities that are unrealized, time wasted. The world disappoints. I was so interested to meet Joseph and hear his story about his nephew. I get it. I understood his frustration with the fact that we each must work out our own lives. What is obvious to one is not necessarily to another." He paused and kissed me. "And I'm so grateful that you and I got on the same page. I mean it, Theresa, I think we are very lucky. Let's not waste it."

I puzzled at how comfortably we fit together. Was I blind to something?

I began to think of writing a young adult book about a girl with a troubled family life who ended up in juvenile court and then learned about designing and building small wooden boats, a girl who blossomed with hidden talents brought to light and who became a role model for others. The illustrations were already forming in my mind, and I was eager to get home to my sketch pad. My publisher had been pestering me for new work, but I'd been too preoccupied with death and change. I felt that our new adventure was restarting my life, as well as Razor's.

He broke my reverie. "Theresa, have you ever heard of a 'push boat'?" He didn't stop for an answer. "We have four of them in the collections at the Chesapeake Bay Maritime Museum. They are modest little boats that were used to push skipjacks on the bay in and out of the harbor as they sailed to the oyster bars for dredging. Skipjacks had them secured with davits over the stern, the bow slightly out of the water. A skipjack under sail is quite a sight—and rare these days. Getting to the oyster grounds became easier when small marine motors were introduced into push boats in the early 20th century. Maryland laws changed, and sail dredging was no longer efficient, but push boats are still used." Razor stopped, and I waited to see where he was going with this information. "I want to be your push boat, Theresa. I want to help you move forward. You are magnificent 'under sail' so to speak, on your own, but I want to help guide you into your full potential. I know you are making major changes that will rebuild your body and your mind. Your spirit doesn't need fixing! I so admire you for your guts, for not accepting what everyone seems to consider normal aging. You are a fighter, and I'm a friend of fighters. Do I sound patronizing?"

"No, you sound wonderful, full of encouragement and conviction. You have given me a boost in more ways than one. Since our time in Alexandria, I have felt stronger and more able. I think we get caught up in common beliefs and expectations and forget to challenge them. We women of a certain age feel a little sorry for ourselves. I've learned that brain health is constantly changing. It needs exercise and building up, and I welcome your help and your watchful eye. My brain is not the boss! I think sometimes deterioration is really just relinquishing hope for the future. You've certainly changed that for me in a most surprising way!"

"Then we are agreed," said Razor, pulling back onto the road. "We are on a mission to strengthen you and strengthen us together along the way. Let's go home and play Bananagrams!"

"Home? Can Whimsy Towers feel like home?" I asked.

"Theresa, from now on, 'home' is where you are. These last few years have just been the waiting room. What are your thoughts about Alexandria?"

"I'm not sure yet. I don't want to sever all aspects of the past too soon. My boy toy might get bored with me."

Razor squeezed my hand. "You don't scare me, and I don't mind the ghosts of your past. Remember, Brad and

I have a living, breathing ghost that may pop up sometime!"

We shared a laugh, but I confess I was curious about the former wife of this man who had landed in my life.

The next few days were filled with Thanksgiving preparation and making space for Razor. I had gotten over the idea of separate bedrooms. I would explain to Tim when he arrived. Fearing the disapproval of one's children is an odd sensation, and their criticism can sneak up like a cat. I was glad for Kevin Jr.'s blessing. Tim was not in a position to discourage sleeping with someone I was not married to. Indiscretion and infidelity are not twins. And immorality is only opinion, shifting in circles of envy. I was not being unfaithful to anyone, and I wondered if he had resolved his marital problems or was resigned to them. His recent visit with Melanie was like a reflection in water that had been disturbed by a stone. I was on guard not to mention it.

Tim and Elizabeth arrived on Tuesday afternoon. The day was gray and gusty, with trees leaning in the wind and shaking their defiant branches. The ocean roiled with angry bursts of temper. It was not a day for outdoor entertaining, and I hoped the weather would warm a bit for Saturday.

Before even removing their suitcases from the rental car, Tim handed me a plain cardboard box.

"You can open this whenever you want," he said, "but perhaps not in front of Elizabeth."

"What is it?"

"It's an apology. You'll understand."

Razor came out of the house, and I handed him the box and introduced him to Elizabeth. She looked frail and unsteady. Her beautiful shiny hair had turned dull, like wooden patio furniture left out too long in the sun. Matted and untamed streaks of gray made me think of Medusa, the once beautiful woman in Greek mythology who was punished by the goddess Athena for actions beyond her control. I hoped Elizabeth had not also been permanently cursed by the alcohol that overpowered and shamed her.

"My dear Elizabeth," I said, as I took her arm and we headed into the house. "It's been too long. I'm so very glad to see you."

"Hi, Razor! How are you?" I heard Tim say behind me. "And congratulations!"

"Congratulations?"

"On the new grandchild. That's great news!"

"Oh, yes. Yes, thanks. There's lots of good news around here."

I looked over my shoulder and saw Razor smiling at me. I think that was the moment I fell in love with my handsome, dark, diplomatic, and daring companion.

Mattie warmed up a blueberry pie while Tim and Elizabeth settled in. She had carefully frozen the abundance of berries from summer and had been pulling them out for smoothies and low sugar pies. She was very strongly onboard with me on reducing sugar in my diet. Mattie was on a subtle journey of reinvention herself and knew the importance of conviction. She no longer made me homemade pralines with South Carolina pecans or swirls of chocolate and peanut butter fudge. Together we made fresh hummus and dug in with sliced red and yellow bell peppers. I ate cashews and almonds instead of chips or candy. Snacks and dessert got new definitions and were satisfying. Processed foods, sugar, and unhealthy cravings were slowly falling away.

I was so happy with the new direction in my life and my decision to be with Razor and was bursting to tell Tim. I wanted to have the conversation before Kev and Brad arrived for dinner. Telling each son separately I hoped would allow for honest response.

In front of a crackling fire that sounded like shards of pottery tumbling in a paper bag, I put my pie aside and began, "Tim, I'm so happy that you and Elizabeth have come. I know it's not an easy trip from South Carolina. I so appreciate it. These last months since losing Dad and David have not been easy for any of us." I glanced at Razor and continued, "Thanks to you and Kev for encouraging me to bring Mattie on full-time. She has been a godsend, and I doubt I would have survived very well without her. She has been the engine that's kept everything running smoothly." I looked over at her, pouring coffee, and took a deep breath. "Recently, however, something else has been added to my life. Razor and I have become close, and he has moved to Whimsy Towers. To be more specific, he has moved in with me this week, into my bedroom. We don't know where this is going, and it's early on several fronts, but it feels like the right step for both of us. I hope this is not too shocking and that you'll be happy for me."

Elizabeth, who was seated closest to the fire, fainted, slumping down in the cushions of her chair.

Tim and Razor jumped to their feet to help her.

"Well, that's not the reaction I'd hoped for!" I said, as the two men lifted her up. She was slow to regain herself. Tim crouched at the side of her chair, holding her hand.

"The traveling has been hard on her," he said. "I wasn't sure we should do it, but she's tried really hard to be strong enough to come. I think I'll take her upstairs. A rest will do her good. I'll be right back."

"May I help?" asked Razor.

"Thanks, but she's light as lace. And by the way, another congratulations!"

Tim returned quickly and came straight over to hug me. "Mom, I think it's wonderful for you, for both of you." His voice cracked as he continued, "Dad would be glad, too. He wanted only your happiness."

My heart burst. I lived the life I had created, and now I could give myself permission to chart a new course, bringing from the past only the indelible imprints that would contribute to the future.

Razor stepped over to shake Tim's hand, and they embraced.

Tim cried openly.

Razor had his hair pulled back in a ponytail. He held my desolate son and let the moment play out. Tim had put a bold face on squandered opportunities. He was a good man in an emotional desert. Disappointment, wrong turns, regret—life overflowed with missteps and wasted time. Tim had made a teenage mistake and spent his adult life trying to make the best of it. Time does not rewind.

As I reached for my coffee, I noticed the tops of my hands and wrists and saw skin like ripples in the sand at low tide.

"Tim, I want you to know that we are not serving alcohol during your visit, even on Thanksgiving. I want to respect and encourage Elizabeth."

"Thanks, Mom, that's thoughtful and appreciated."

"Shall I open the mystery box?"

Tim managed a laugh. "Oh, yes. This is a good time."

Razor handed me the box, and I opened it with a gasp. On top of crumpled paper was the small silver baby cup missing from the dining room. As I dug deeper, I found the Herend figurines that had also gone missing. Each was wrapped with care. There was no note or explanation.

"Have you guessed?" asked Tim.

"I can guess," answered Razor. I turned to him in total disbelief and curiosity.

"Melanie," was his simple response.

"Melanie?" I exclaimed. "Melanie?"

Tim nodded.

"She gave us a hint when she talked about being an 'e-Bay entrepreneur.' She resells things online," Razor continued. "She sells little things that ship easily, perhaps things she can find in homes that she can drop in her handbag and might not be missed. On a day busy with a crowd of people you did not know, she was able to deflect attention and suspicion. And she may have observed that you were not at full mental or physical capacity and may not notice."

"I cannot believe it!" I leaned back and laughed. "Tim, did I mention that Razor was a career CIA officer?" For the first time, I wondered if my resident sleuth would sometime ferret out my own secrets.

"I'm so sorry, Mom. I didn't know she had taken the things. A couple of months later, Melanie told me that she was pregnant. I knew she wanted to have a child, that her mysterious female clock was ticking, and I dreaded the thought that I might be the father. We weren't too careful."

"Oh, Tim, here we go again!"

"I know, I'm a slow learner, but she was like.... "

"Like a drug you couldn't refuse," I said.

"Yes, like a tonic that stirred my life and made me whole. I regret to say like a conqueror of some kind. She liked to tempt me to madness and then submit."

"Not too many details, please," I said, remembering their encounter on the chair.

"The thing is, she said she'd had unprotected sex with different men and didn't know who the father was, and she wasn't going to find out with DNA. She didn't want anything from any of us, just the child."

"So why return the goods?" I asked.

"She was here when Dad died and actually wanted to put the things back, but realized how obvious that would be. She said she felt guilty that she had stolen from you during such a terrible time of loss, that you had been so welcoming and kind. And you would be the grand-mother of her baby, if our lovemaking produced one."

"A thief with selective conscience," said Razor, shak-ing his head with a smile.

"I guess so," answered Tim. "I haven't seen her since she delivered the box to my office. She said she just couldn't sell the things. I didn't know she had multiple partners. I had felt special, exclusive, wanted."

"And duped?" I added.

"Don't be too hard on him, Theresa," Razor said. Then he shifted to his investigative nature, "Will you try to determine paternity?"

"I'm not sure how," Tim answered.

"Oh, there are lots of ways to get a sample after the child is born," answered the retired professional. "Lots of ways."

The subject hung in the air, with no one to catch it. Was knowing the father a choice, an obligation, a curi-osity? I had nothing to contribute to the topic of pater-nity, and Tim had not fully grasped it.

Brad and Kev arrived for dinner with an alert Charles David. He'd been fed and bathed and dressed up for meeting his aunt and uncle. Someone had knitted him a warm cap that had rabbit ears, and they flopped into his face, causing him to blink and shake his head.

"Wait till the day he wrestles control over his own wardrobe!" I said as I took Charlie from Brad. "He will not thank you for sartorial silliness."

Kev laughed and answered, as he hugged his brother, "I figure there will be many categories of criticism to face; maybe baby clothes will not register. How are you, Tim? How's Elizabeth?"

I handed Charles David to Tim as he answered, "It's been a long day. Elizabeth is resting, but we're both so glad to be here to celebrate with you tomorrow. A marriage, a baby, Thanksgiving, a party—it's a holiday package we could not refuse."

Tim looked down intently at his tiny nephew, still swaddled in blankets, and repeated his name, "Charles David. Charles David. What a nice reason for remembering. David would love it."

I gazed at my two sons next to Razor and his son, these diverse and caring men who would help me shape my future. Loneliness is a path we often choose by mistake, for lack of seeing other options. Or pursuing them.

"And what about this new relationship?" continued Tim, smiling at Razor and me. "Shall we take a vote on this radical behavior? Really, Mother, the grieving widow has abandoned her widow's weeds and weeping veil rather soon. Your sons are mortified."

"Yes," continued Kev, "We don't know who should say 'Welcome' to whom. You're jumbling up both families together. And it's great. Shall we have a toast?"

"Thank you, but no toasting. We are trying to be mindful of Elizabeth," I answered. "The rule does not, of course, apply to your party on Saturday, just here with the family. And Razor knows that there is still mourning going on, even if I'm not wearing black for a Victorian year. He has opened a new door, but the old one has not yet completely closed."

"I'm a man with a long view," he interjected, reaching for my hand, "and there is enough encouragement for me along the way. I'm content with that."

"Have you ever been with a man whose hair was longer than yours, Mom?"

"No, smarty-pants, but at least he's older than my children," I managed to say before Razor drew me into his arms and sealed the debate with a kiss, a kiss that lingered like honey melting into warm tea.

Chapter Twenty-Three

"Razor, when do you think we make the mental shift away from believing that everything is still ahead of us in life?" I asked, waking fully to see a man in my bed, his breathing soft and close.

"I plan never to make that shift," he answered, pulling me into him. My nightgown had disappeared in the night. "Yesterday should not impede our tomorrows. We have lots of fields to plow before sunset."

"Do you feel a little bit naughty, here with me, with all of our children and grandson under this roof?"

"As long as they're not in this room, I'm thrilled," he replied, pushing back my hair and then his. "I have not a speck of guilt." For at least half an hour, there was no further conversation.

The aroma of coffee gradually wafted its way into our room. We threw on robes and followed the smell of sausage and coffee to the kitchen. It looked like a slumber party, with no one dressed for the day except Mattie. Kev was turning sausages and bacon, and Elizabeth sat with Charlie, as Brad helped Mattie set the table and pour juice.

"What a wonderful sight!" I said. "What a wonderful family."

"And what a wonderful day," continued Kev. "Let's have a wedding!"

We all laughed, and Razor squeezed my hand as he looked at me with a prescient stare.

I was beginning to see a happy ending for this story of romance and surprise: two strangers blown together by a wind that held its breath until the bigger storm had passed. Calm was settling on my tortured conscience. Could Razor accept me with secrets? Could I accept me with secrets?

He held my hand during the entire marriage ceremony, as we watched our two sons enter solemnly into a pact that we no longer shared: death and divorce, the grim reapers of marital success. I now had two unconventional, or nonconventional, married sons. One had responded to duty and responsibility more than choice; the other chose nontraditional and unapologetic love. I shed tears of happiness and gratitude for them and for my own marriage, which had been a bulwark against fatal attraction. I had not thought of Rick in a romantic way in many years, but he was the path not taken, and I gave thanks for his part in steering me home.

The plan was for Brad and Kev to have a night off on their own after the ceremony, while the army of baby sitters at Whimsy Towers took Charlie duty. We braced ourselves for a sleepless night before Thanksgiving.

Razor congratulated Brad and Kev and announced that he had an errand to run on the way home. "I'll see you in a bit," he said, kissing my cheek without explanation.

Mattie had prepared a buffet of seafood and salads, steamed vegetables and cabbage soup with clams. Cheese biscuits were fresh from the oven. Charles David was happy as long as someone held him, and I noticed that he did not shake as much as previously, even when lying alone on a blanket. His little body was still fighting a mighty battle with the unintentional present his mother had given him. Opioids were ruining families everywhere, killing a hundred people a day in the US, but his new parents kept their eye on the future. Charles David would have a future.

As we gathered to begin serving ourselves dinner in the dining room, chatting about the afternoon, Razor arrived with a jubilant expression and a cat carrier.

"Theresa, I've brought you something for Thanksgiving."

He opened the soft flap and lifted out a calico cat.

"When we were in St. Michaels at the museum, you said you were about ready for an old dog or a cat. I'm offering you both. I'm the 'old dog,' and here is a cat. Her name is Grace. Her owner has moved to a nursing home and was not allowed to take a pet with her. She needed a home."

He gently handed me Grace, and she settled into my arms as if she'd always been there.

"Oh, Razor, she is beautiful! What a wonderful gift. I love her."

"And she comes trained—unlike the 'old dog'—but we're all learning together."

"I'm happy with the 'old dog' as he comes," I replied. "I think he's trained just fine."

Grace was not startled by the enthusiasm, the multiple hands that wanted to pet her, or the squeals of a baby who was momentarily neglected. She personified her name.

"I miss having an animal around, and Grace is a welcome addition to my evolving family. Thank you so much."

"Your evolving collection of orphans," quipped Razor, winking at me. "I've offered to bring Grace for visitation in the parking lot of the nursing home. The woman had her for eight years, and the separation has been difficult."

"How did you find her?" Elizabeth asked, trying to comfort Charlie, as Mattie handed her a warm bottle for him. "I doubt the Humane Society would give out that much information."

"No, this was a private adoption!" Razor paused, obviously deciding how much more to disclose. "I went back down the beach to talk with Joseph." Looking at Tim and Elizabeth, he continued, "He's a man we met not long ago. He has a nephew that's of interest to me. Joseph had taken custody of the cat. The woman is his friend, and she didn't want Grace to go in a cage and be gawked at. Joseph is a very thoughtful guy and agreed to keep Grace if he couldn't find a proper home."

Mattie stood still, intent on the story about Joseph. Razor added, "It was my idea to take her for occasional visits, a little like joint custody. I hope you don't mind."

"Oh my, no, of course not," I said quickly. "One thing we know for sure around here is the value of accumulated connections. 'One thing leads to another' is a trite expression loaded with truth."

"I'm glad you like her," he said. "She seems easy to have around, the independent cat thing, without too many demands. The previous owner has had her since she was a kitten. And one thing did lead to another. Joseph wants to take me to meet her. He's been talking to her about creating a program on the Cape for youth who want to learn carpentry and woodworking, maybe boat building, and she'd like to finance it. She has no heirs and wants to leave some kind of local legacy. She's a widow who lost her only child years ago. Joseph has been looking out for her. How's that for serendipity?"

"This is a day of such terrific news!" I exclaimed. "Joseph impressed me with his sincerity and seriousness. I liked him, and he sounds like the gateway to a new adventure. Your talents and interests might find a home together here. Are you ready for that kind of commitment?"

Razor looked at me as if I was the only person in the room. "My interests are already finding a home here, and I'm very ready for the commitment."

I realized that my life was a jumble of minutiae that needed to be sorted out and realigned with others'. Details pile up. Some changes I could not control, only the response to them, but choices determine direction. We are what we let in, what shapes our thinking. I couldn't see any dark clouds on the horizon and basked in the wonder of it.

"Now we have even more to celebrate," I announced, adding a cheese biscuit to my plate of healthy vegetables. "This is turning into a very good Thanksgiving after all."

Grace accepted her new home with purposeful exploration, going from room to room. When we settled down to eat, she settled into a sofa with soft cushions under a window. I wondered if she knew the morning sun would fill that space with light.

"Susan and her parents are coming for Thanksgiving tomorrow, but if anyone has tricks or stories to tell about Kev and Brad, now's the time to plan. There will be lots of people we don't know at their party on Saturday."

"We could hide their baby and see if they could find him," said Tim. "We could make up clues, like a treasure hunt."

Razor and I looked at each other and then at Mattie, and we burst into laughter.

"A missing baby does not sound like a good trick," I answered, without explaining our reaction. "Let's not create a crisis. How about something less anxiety-driven?"

"I could invite Brad's mother," Razor offered, smiling.

"I suggested *less* anxiety-driven!" I could not imagine becoming a grandmother and being denied access to my only grandchild, and secretly I wished I could see the woman Razor had spent so many years with. Maybe someday she would find a way back into the lives of the men who left her behind.

"Any mischievous, but *constructive* ideas?"

"We'll sleep on it," answered Tim.

Sleep, however, was not the order of the day, or rather, the night. Charles David had a hard time getting through the hours that stretched on like a ball game in extra innings. We all took shifts, helping each other with varying jobs to feed and console the struggling child whose body did not give him peace. Mattie's singing was the best comfort. She rocked and sang her Sunday best to him, providing long periods of calm.

In the morning, I was still hearing bits of her gentle Appalachian lullaby in my head:

> *Bright morning stars are rising*
> *Bright morning stars are rising*
> *Bright morning stars are rising*
> *Day is a'breaking in my soul.*

Thanksgiving arrived with brilliant sunshine, canceling the gray of previous days. The metaphor was not lost on me, and a specific day for giving thanks was a subtle reminder to do it every day. Past sadness was not an albatross.

Charles David was all smiles and happiness. When his parents arrived, we downplayed the fretful night and gave thanks for the chance of spending time with him.

I was holding and tickling Charlie in front of the fire when I saw Susan coming to the door. Rick was behind her, and I met them at the door.

"Where's your mother? I hope she's well."

"She is well, but she's gone."

"Gone? Gone where?"

Rick continued. "She's left. The college eliminated her classes, and she's not been happy for awhile. She's gone back to Germany."

"For how long?"

"I don't think she's coming back," Susan said, her eyes filling with tears.

I put my arms around this beautiful young woman who seemed to be facing loss every time I saw her. She looked exhausted and depleted.

"Well, I'm so glad you've come to be with us today."

Every generation molds its own traditions, and holidays have always been important affairs at Whimsy Towers. Thanksgiving afternoon was for TV football and relaxation; dinner was for coming together and conversation. I loved it all, but a dreary pall settled over Rick and his daughter, keeping them at a distance.

When it was time to eat, we all walked into the dining room together and found places to sit. I wasn't paying attention where anyone settled.

Mattie had organized the catering help, and dinner was all elegance, served with Theodosia's best china and silver. Enormous arrangements of greenery with red berries accented the serving stations. The room smelled of spiced candles, pine, and roasted turkey.

I stared at the large portrait of my mother and grandmother and felt Susan's sorrow. When the small light under the picture was turned on, I sometimes thought their eyes were following me. Mothers and daughters was a complicated dance. I could only watch it from a distance.

ACT THREE

RICK: I'm sorry we've brought gloom to this special occasion. We are both really so glad for you and Brad, Kev. Tell us how your lives have changed.

Kev stands and lifts his water glass.

KEV: I would like to salute and toast my best friend and now husband, who has changed my life in so many good ways, including drawing me into the adventure of being a parent. And I include in this toast a nod to my mother, whom I now know had a forever challenging, nonstop job in being a parent. Doing this twice would take some serious fortitude!

Everyone laughs and toasts. Theresa stands and blows a kiss to her son.

BRAD: We thank you all for taking Charlie last night. I know some nights are harder than others, but he is truly getting better. We haven't slept through the night yet, but we know there is progress, and progress fuels our hope for the future.
RAZOR: Amen to that.

Theresa looks quizzically at Razor and smiles.

THERESA: Susan, are you sure your mother is not coming back? Maybe she just needs a break. Parents do, at any age. She's been here over thirty years. What's left for her in Germany?

SUSAN: She wants to live in her own language. She stayed to say goodbye when I arrived home this week, but she was already packed and determined. Can you imagine walking out on your child?

RICK: I think she figured you were grown and on your own.

BRAD: Well, my mother walked out on me without going anywhere! She could not accept me and insisted I become someone I was not in order to have her love.

TIM: Sounds as though she does not love you less, Susan, just from a distance.

Razor stares intently at Tim, who is seated across the table next to Rick.

ELIZABETH: My mother lives nearby, yet is unable to function very well as a mother, wife, or anything. I think sometimes we just give in to forces that try to pull us off track, and we lose our way. I wish I were stronger in my own convictions, more on guard. I think your mother is not damaged, like mine, Susan, just weary, and weary can be refreshed.

Elizabeth looks down. Tim reaches for her hand and smiles at her.

RICK: We'll figure this out somehow. *Jugaad.* Maybe we will be a family in transit. It's hard to give up. *Jugaad* is a Hindi word for thinking outside the box, improvising a solution. Even a temporary answer can lead to something good that lasts. I'm learning again that what I expected to be forever has no guarantees. And I'm not the first one at this table to find out that marriage is not a smooth run. Kev and Brad, we hope you stay on course—and wish you well!

THERESA: Here, here! And now I have some news. Mattie has agreed to take a course with me at the college on Ireland and Irish film. I admit she is a reluctant participant, but I've assured her that we will stick together. I think it won't be easy for either of us.

This week we received some preliminary information, articles about the potato famine, rural romanticism, emigration, and a wonderful poem entitled "Spraying the Potatoes" by Irish poet Patrick Kavanagh. We've been reading the poem aloud to each other to get in the mood, and we're both feeling excited about going back to class and heading to Ireland without leaving home.

RAZOR: Mattie, are your fears melting away?

MATTIE: I feel not all stupid. Talkin' about language makes me speak better language. That's a big goal for me. Talkin' is how we understand another person. What's in my head is clear, but what comes out the mouth needs some improving. I can hear the words I fall down on.

THERESA: You are definitely on your way, and you are definitely not stupid. Mattie, you are smart and have good instincts. I think we will have a great time in our class, encouraging each other. The first movie we're going to see is "The Quiet Man," and believe it or not, it stars John Wayne! It sounds like a bit of a contrived love story from the 1950s, but Ireland is the point. Mattie and I will report back.

ELIZABETH: I'm rather jealous of you both, an opportunity to explore another country and culture through film. I'd like to try to tackle something like that.

TIM: Maybe we could find a similar program at the local college back home. We could do it together.

Everyone resumes eating. Servers move around the table. Brad stands.

BRAD: Kev and I really appreciate your good wishes and everyone celebrating with us today, and we hope to see you all on Saturday at the party, but I want us to take a moment to remember those who are not here this Thanksgiving. I add Susan's mother to the list of those missed, but I want especially to remember Kev's father and brother, two wonderful men who left us too soon.

The older I get, the more importance I see in role models. I had, and have, a terrific father. He stood up for me, believed in me, and wants to share in my happiness. I'm so grateful for you, Dad. Kev has lost his father, and something will always be missing for him. Charles David will also feel that loss. So on this day of giving thanks, let's remember Kevin and David and be grateful that they touched our lives and remain in our hearts.

TIM: To Dad and David. We miss you.

SUSAN: To my darling David.

THERESA: To Kevin and David, love always.

Everyone stands. Razor stares at Tim and then at Rick.

Chapter Twenty-Four

Thanksgiving is like a gift for the soul from contemporary culture trying to be generous. It's a day for blinders, when scars are covered with kisses. I gave thanks for what truly were my blessings and could disregard the preponderance of mistakes and regret. For one day, I could hide in gestures. Gratitude is safe harbor. We lay out our unguarded optimism in thanks with no need to balance the ingratitude we live.

Thanksgiving has a dubious history. We celebrate feasting with Native Americans to whom we lied, cheated, gave diseases, displaced, and ultimately slaughtered. Conquerors rewrite and reinterpret facts to assuage missteps. Repeating what we want to believe gradually makes it real. Politicians do it; I do it. Unchallenged, we remain in our own contented bubble.

I hope my failures are behind me. Thanksgiving is one of the heart's best cover-ups, but it comes with a hangover. The next day is a sober trip back to reality.

Elizabeth was outside having a morning cigarette when I spotted her bundled up on the patio couch, stroking a sleeping Grace. The cat was curled up next to her on a sunny cushion that mirrored the orange and black colors of her fur.

"I didn't know you smoked."

"I don't often, but it helps distract me from wanting a drink. You are kind to keep my temptation out of sight. It poisons more than my body. I know I have caused Tim a lot of pain. Being with your family this week, and away from my mother and her drinking, has really helped. Thank you, Theresa. I'm so glad that we made the trip, and I'm sorry I could not be here for David's funeral."

"Tim loves you, Elizabeth, and wants to do whatever will help."

"I wanted love to be the answer," she replied, "but love has not been strong enough, and I seem unable to claim my life."

"Each day fits like a piece of life's puzzle, Liz. They cannot be forced and sometimes find their way together slowly, but eventually they form a complete picture, if you keep trying. My analogy has its weaknesses, but it reinforces the possibilities. You and Tim deserve a purposeful life, a complete life, a relationship based on trust and respect. There is hope in that."

"Do you know he cheats on me?"

I wasn't sure how to respond, and she continued. "He thinks I don't know, but I'm not drunk *all* the time. Odd phone calls, unexpected out-of-town trips, lingering fragrance. A man living deceit needs to mind the details. Tim is too trusting and naïve; he wasn't made for deception, but I cannot denigrate him. The contempt I feel is for myself. His infidelity is really a product of my own failure." She paused and said softly, "We all want someone to think we matter."

I sat down next to her and wrapped my arms around her slender body. She smelled of smoke.

Mattie came out to the patio with a tray of glasses. She was beginning set-up preparation for the party the next day. "It's chilly out here. How about some coffee?" she asked.

"Oh, yes, please," I answered. "It's wonderful here in the sunshine, and I hope it stays warm enough for tomorrow. We can squeeze everyone into the house, but I never tire of the view from here."

Clouds meandered across the sky in clumps heading out to sea. The brilliance of sunrise caressing the ocean had melted into the new day, spreading its light in a larger embrace. We sat in silence with our thoughts.

"Hello, ladies," announced Razor, as he stepped outside and approached us. "I'm the coffee delivery for Mattie."

"Wonderful. Please join us," I answered.

"Thank you, but I'm going to find Tim," said Elizabeth. "I'd like a walk down the beach before breakfast. I'm feeling steady enough. Thanks for our talk, Theresa. See you both later."

Mattie was waiting for the full measure of faces to serve breakfast. Brad, Kev, and Charlie had gone home after dinner, but the rest of us straggled downstairs like intermittent mail delivery. Mattie was a master juggler, ready to receive and accommodate us when she had collected the crowd.

"Did I interrupt something?" Razor asked.

"No, but Elizabeth knows that Tim cheats on her. He's blissfully ignorant of her knowledge. Why does he think he can get away with that?"

Razor did not comment. He sipped his coffee, looking pensive.

"Theresa, infidelity is a complicated business. Moral indifference is not generally the reason. People choose to cheat. I think it's even possible to cheat for love."

"How can that be?" I asked.

"You cannot guess?"

I froze in my seat, fearful of the conversation to come. Razor did not look unkind, just thoughtful and determined. I felt suddenly alone and acutely in charge of my own life, my own puzzle.

"Well, last night I sat across the table from Tim. He was seated next to Rick. There are curious physical similarities between them and especially in their mannerisms, even their speech patterns and inflection. They are very at ease with each other, which is natural and wonderful for family friends, but is there something more? Is there something you want to tell me about the rough road to parenthood for you and Kevin?"

"I don't know what you mean."

"I think you do. Theresa, I'm trained to see truth in impossibilities and impossibility in what seems to be truth. If we are to have any kind of serious relationship, we need to be honest with each other."

"You think Tim is not my child?"

"No, I think he's not Kevin's child. Which also brings to mind Kev Jr. and his marriage to my son. Biology and genes will not directly dictate their future together, or Charlie's, but honesty does. I only met the boys' father that one day, at David's funeral, and I liked him. He was a good man, a good father; but Theresa, don't let us begin with a lie. Lying is the fountain of misery."

I took a deep breath and frantically considered my choices, weighing loss and gain. I gripped my coffee mug so it would not slip from my hand. I felt my face turn hot.

"That's outrageous!" I blurted out. "How could you think that?"

Razor stared at me, not in anger or hostility, but in wonderment.

"Theresa, you came here alone during a time you were struggling in your marriage. You and Kevin both wanted the children that nature had denied you together. I think another option surfaced, perhaps by mistake at first, then by longing or even love. I do not want to judge, but I do want the truth."

"I have nothing else to say."

Razor put down his coffee mug and stood.

"I'm going to pack up and head to Brad and Kev's. I'll be back for the party tomorrow with them and then drive home to Maryland."

His use of the word "home" for Maryland pierced my heart. Part of me wanted to fling myself at his feet and beg forgiveness, to lay my transgressions in the open; and part of me needed to keep hiding the truth, which would inevitably expand to include David's death and the chance I might have participated in it. Moral courage eluded me. I had obliterated the possibility of facing the future in grateful reprieve.

My inner secret had been spoken. It was now embedded in the woodwork, in the air that held other secrets at Whimsy Towers.

Tim and Elizabeth walked from the house through the back screened porch and headed toward the beach. They wore warm coats, probably heavier than what was ever necessary in South Carolina. Tim had his arm around his wife, and he occasionally stopped and drew her into him for a long kiss. They soon disappeared from my view, and I was left in the rut of private remorse.

⚘

"I don't want to leave without saying goodbye," Razor said as he came outside with several suitcases and a duffel bag. "I think we need some mental and physical space, perhaps a reality check. At least we made no false promises." His eyes were red. "I'll miss you, Theresa. I confess this is a miserable, sad day. I'll see you tomorrow. Let's make it about our sons and not get into our sinking ship."

"Oh, Razor, I ...." But he walked quickly to his car.

Mattie arrived with a breakfast tray for me. "I think we're doin' this in bits today. Too much comin' and goin'. No telling if we'll finish breakfast before lunchtime!" Scrambled eggs with cheese and ham looked delicious, and I did not question Mattie on where she'd gotten the cinnamon bun dripping with warm butter.

"Is everything coming together for the party?" I asked, eager to deflect my mood.

"Oh, yes, they got people calling and makin' plans for food, chairs, and music. This house is going to see quite a party." She paused. "Excuse me, but is everything all right?"

"No, it is not," I replied without explanation. "It definitely is not."

I retreated to poetry in my head. Mathew Arnold ended his poem "Dover Beach" with my feelings. It is a lonely, lyrical journey of disappointment:

> *Ah, love, let us be true*
> *To one another! For the world, which seems*
> *To lie before us like a land of dreams,*
> *So various, so beautiful, so new,*
> *Hath really neither joy, nor love, nor light,*
> *Nor certitude, nor peace, nor help for pain;*
> *And we are here as on a darkling plain*
> *Swept with confused alarms of struggle and flight,*
> *Where ignorant armies clash by night.*

The retreating power of love and the loss of peace on a *"darkling plain"* made me feel deeply the emptiness of life without Razor. The world cannot keep promises, but poetry can move us from the indicative to the imperative. I had more than gotten used to Razor; I relied on him, I cared for him. I wondered if the battle was over, *"Swept with confused alarms of struggle and flight."* I wondered if hope was lost.

In the middle of these musings, I heard a car coming down the driveway. It was Rick. For an instant, I remembered his long-ago visits and the way my heart and whole body stirred at the sight of him. Razor's surmise brought that intimacy back from history, the anxious desire, the physical satisfaction.

ⓒⱬ

"Hi, Theresa, I wanted to apologize for our brittle behavior yesterday. We were in quite a funk. We're still sorting things out, of course, but Susan has gone back to D.C. and sends apologies for missing the party tomorrow. And I wanted to come see you alone."

"Rick, you were nice to come yesterday, dealing with such a shock. Coffee?"

"No, thanks. Is this a good time?"

"A good time for what?"

He sat next to me on the couch, and the cat jumped down to find more settled accommodation.

"Theresa, I see this as a crossroads, and we've been there before. We are no longer young and hesitant, trying to deny what was between us. Years ago, you felt guilty and disloyal with a living husband, and I with a deceased wife. We tried to deny our feelings, but it just didn't work. We could not stop the desire. Now those obstacles are gone, and with my wife leaving me, we are both free. I've come to see if there is still the spark that could rekindle. I know it's soon after Kevin's death, but, Theresa, I don't want to lose you again."

My jaw dropped. "Rick, do you think these rickety old bones can still roll on the carpet? We are different people. Our families have become such good friends. Our children are friends."

"That makes it all the more possible and reasonable. Our families already feel combined, and I doubt those old bones have totally retired. We have always had more than a physical connection."

He smiled and took both my hands in his, and I was surprised I felt a surge of emotion. Perhaps it was memory. His hands were warm as he lifted mine to his lips and kissed them.

"Is it dead between us? Can we finally have the future that we denied ourselves thirty-five years ago?" He laughed. "You know, I've had a younger wife all these years to keep the juices active."

"You are shameful!" I exclaimed, pulling my hands away and laughing at him.

"Yes, I am, but not ashamed. I have feelings for you that are deep and honest. There is no dishonor in new beginnings."

"And what if your wife wakes up and comes back?"

"I do still love her." Rick looked down briefly, and I saw the depth of his hurt in his furrowed brow and tired face. "We've had a wonderful life together, and she's the mother of my child, but I think she means it. She's gone. I'm not rushing you, Theresa. Or me. Time needs to heal wounds for both of us. I want us to get reacquainted in a new way, or maybe in an old way." He laughed again and kissed my cheek, which he had done countless times in our last decades as friends. "We have some catching up to do."

Tim and Elizabeth appeared on the lawn and came toward the patio, where we sat.

"This looks cozy," Tim said, as they reached us, with red cheeks and smiles. "We should light up the fire pit Rick built for us in the garden when we were kids. Marshmallows for breakfast, anyone?"

"No," Elizabeth teased, looking fondly at her husband and poking his arm. "We've had a wonderful walk on a beautiful, crisp day. I feel tougher and resilient here. Tim and I have been able to talk some things through this morning. I feel really happy—and ready for serious food. Serious food follows serious conversation. Both are good."

I wondered what she meant but did not pursue it. I had serious conversation of my own to contemplate and sort through. I had two men taking off and landing in my life like planes on an aircraft carrier.

"Two for breakfast?" Mattie asked as she came to pick up my tray and refill the coffee.

Tim answered. "Yes, thank you, Mattie, we're definitely ready for breakfast. We'll come inside where it's warmer, and we'd like to help you prepare for the party. Have you got Razor somewhere on a project this morning?"

She looked at me and then said, "Nothing really much to do. It's mostly out of my hands."

"Mine, too," I added, as I held up my cup for a refill.

Chapter Twenty-Five

I think there's a reason that roots are buried, out of sight. They're not meant to be dug up and analyzed. The plant or tree grows from its own upward need. Reaching for sunshine is the impetus. Perhaps I have refused to be my best self, like paint slowly chipping off the storm door, but I'm hoping that disciplined thinking will re-shape my mind and lead to new direction and living. I do not want to leave just a memoir of mistakes and tragedy.

Kev and Brad arrived mid-morning to help organize their party. Mattie was happy to relinquish all other duties for the opportunity to take care of Charles David. She eagerly whisked him away, and the last sound we heard as she headed out the kitchen door was singing: *"Hush, little baby, don't you cry, ..."*

Without her telling me directly, I knew that Mattie often slipped down the beach to visit Joseph. Taking the baby for a walk would provide a good excuse, if indeed she still needed one.

I suddenly felt sad that Razor's plans of working with Joseph on a program for troubled youth would now evaporate. He would doubtless stay in St. Michaels and only visit the Cape occasionally to see his son and grandson. I was in mourning all over again.

Tim found me outside on the lawn, seated under an umbrella close to the boathouse. I loved sitting near the ocean, feeling its mist in every season and hearing the insistent sound of waves crashing into whatever was in its way. The ocean did not compromise. Its routine was fixed by its own whim.

"Hi, Mom. Do you need anything? Are you warm enough?"

"I'm fine, thanks, Tim. I'm so happy right here. I feel connected to this devious, plotting ocean, conspiring to challenge our vulnerabilities. The ocean always wins." I took a deep breath and exhaled slowly. "I'm really glad you and Elizabeth made the trip. I know it was not easy. Do you think she's doing all right?"

"Yes, we've had a terrific time, and I confess I rather dread going back, returning to a familiar routine that sometimes threatens and overwhelms us both. Being here is a little like hiding from our life. I wonder if we should leave South Carolina. Her mother would probably spiral out of control, and her father would be devastated, but her well-being is number one. I want to deal better with that. I've told her I want to be a better support, more engaged, more loving and faithful. I don't want her to feel alone."

"Is that the conversation you had on the beach yesterday?"

"Yes, avoidance is no longer working for me. I finally feel dirty and dishonest and no longer justified in my betrayals. I confessed my infidelity to Liz, and do you know what?"

"She already knew."

"Yes, she did. How did you know that?"

"She told me. And she felt it was her fault, not yours."

"Oh, Mother," said Tim, kneeling next to my chair and breaking into tears, "I do love her. How can I atone? How do I regain lost trust?"

"My darling son, I cannot advise you, but I do know that good intentions can pave the road going forward. What is past is not fixable, only redeemable. Liz loves you. Build on that."

We sat together in silence, watching the ocean churn in frolicking waves that stumbled onto the rocks.

"Would you like me to put the things from Melanie back into the dining room?" Tim asked.

"Yes, thank you. Let's get ourselves back to normal!" And I silently wondered what "normal" was.

The party began as the sun hit its midday height. Guests eased from the house and the patio out onto the lawn and even strolled the beach. The band played under the awning, but few people danced. It was a day for drinking and toasting. I kept an eye on Elizabeth. Tim was by her side except when he occasionally joined his brother.

Razor neither drank nor ate. He looked like a lawn ornament, and I had never before seen him so downcast and disconnected. At one point, he lifted a glass and made a beautiful toast to Brad and Kev and Charlie, expressing the joy of new generations and the promise and importance of love, but I noticed the glass did not even touch his lips. For a few moments, he rose eloquently to the occasion, but to me he seemed present in body but absent in spirit. I wanted to go and wrap my arms around this caring man who had been blindsided. He did not deserve it. I did not deserve him.

As the afternoon wore on, Razor came up to me, carrying our sleeping grandson.

"I'm going to head out soon. I need to get on the road, but I want to leave with only good feelings between us. Theresa, this little guy will bring us together for many years ahead, and I don't want it to be awkward. My feelings for you have not changed, but the possibilities have. Brad and Kev have both asked me what's happened. They're really concerned. I told them that we were rushing into something that didn't have time to build a solid foundation, which I hope is true enough."

"And they believed that?"

He laughed, and I was glad to see the first sign of that familiar smile as he continued, "No, they did not!"

"I'll be on guard to give a believable story," I replied.

He looked at me with a quizzical expression. "Devising fabrication?"

"Razor, I told you in the beginning that I had a complicated and muddled past."

"Complicated is workable; lack of trust is not. Can you not believe that I care enough about you to work through the labyrinth of your past, mistakes and all?"

I felt as though I'd been stripped naked, standing bare in front of a crowd of onlookers. Razor was offering me a warm blanket, and I could not accept it.

"Well, until the next time," he said, gently handing me Charles David.

I stood alone in the middle of the sweeping lawn, tears sliding down my face.

"Hey, Mom! Mom!" called Kev. "We need you over here. We want to take a picture before Razor leaves. We want a picture of all of us together."

Razor and I stood at opposite ends of a smiling family. Phone cameras snapped, and I wished I were a phantasm that could not be captured on film.

The afternoon was beginning to cool, and as guests began to leave, Rick approached me for the first time that day. He looked troubled, and I had noticed that he hadn't arrived until the party was well underway.

"Is everything okay?" I asked, directly avoiding the conversation of the day before.

"I'm not sure."

"Rick, you caught me off guard yesterday. I did not mean to be rude."

"Oh, no, it's not that." He hesitated, as if sorting through a chain of events that was still unraveling. "And you were not rude. We've known each other too long to play games or get offended. I was nervous and excited about what might lie ahead for both of us after all these years, but they have been good years, happy years." He struggled to continue. "I had a phone call in the middle of the night from Germany. She is still mixed up about the time zones." He tried to laugh. "She's happy to be back in her old familiar life, the culture of her childhood, and is settling in, but...."

I waited in silence to see where he was leading me.

"She was in tears, Theresa. Just sobbing on the phone, already missing Susan and me. She said she could not come back and begged me to join her in Germany. I'm retiring at the end of this semester, and we had talked about different ideas for the future, but Germany was not one of them. She hasn't been gone a week, and it's all up in the air again. I don't know what to do."

I hugged my dear friend. "Rick, integrity has been a pretty good guide for you, as I recall." We both laughed, and I looked into his blue eyes and noticed for the first time how they had faded with the years. We are no longer those young lovers who once wanted to share every minute, every dream, every part of our bodies. Aging had chained the impulses of youth and given in return the freedom and grace of propriety.

"Would it help you to know that I cannot make a romantic plan for going forward? I have too many issues to sort out, but there will always be a special bond between us and a memory that cannot be taken away. I have no regrets about that."

"Did you ever tell Kevin about us? I've often wondered."

"No, I never told him," I said, looking down briefly, hiding the truth that still needed to be hidden from Rick. "And if he suspected I was unfaithful during those summers, he never confronted me. Kevin and I both mellowed over time. He was grateful for his family and the life we had. I'm glad you and he became good friends."

Geese flew low overhead, en route to warmth. "I miss him," I continued, and hugged Rick again. "Go to her, Rick. Follow your instincts and keep your family intact. It's the difficult choice I made so many years ago, and it was the right one for me. It's not always the right choice, but it sounds as though your heart is urging you in the same direction of not giving up on someone you do truly care about. What does Susan think?"

"We had a long talk this morning. She's a very able adult on her own, but she hopes the family will stay together. I am torn."

"Then why not just try it? Pull up stakes and have an overseas adventure. Your German is pretty good. Think of it as a semester abroad, an immersion into a different culture. It may reactivate your marriage to be in new surroundings, freshen things up."

"I've always enjoyed your answers to stale living!"

"Well, they have changed over time!" We both laughed. "But I still see the need to question, to explore, to test what gets too familiar and routine. Maybe your marriage just needs replanting in different soil to grow differently. I hope you won't abandon it before trying."

"Theresa, may I tell you that I love you? And I don't mean in a grasping, urgent, physical way. I love that you've been in my life."

"Yes, I understand, and I love you back. We are stuck with each other in many wonderful ways, even if you're living in Germany."

Rick was the last guest to leave the party. Brad and Kev had wanted to get home to feed Charles David, and

252 | ANN HYMES

Mattie and the servers were cleaning up outside. Tim was folding chairs, and I asked him where Elizabeth was.

"She went inside awhile ago to lie down. She's feeling pretty depressed about going home tomorrow, but I haven't seen her touch a drop of alcohol today. I think this ocean air and being with our family has given her strength that she feels slipping away at the prospect of returning to South Carolina. We've got to make some changes. And soon."

"Do you want to stay on here awhile? I won't be going back to Alexandria for several weeks and may even stay here for Christmas. My plans have changed, too."

"Do you want to talk about it, Mom? Razor looked miserable. What happened?"

"I need to sit down," I answered. Tim offered his arm, and we walked slowly to the screened porch. The emotions of the day were catching up with me.

"You know Kev and I were happy for you, don't you?"

"Oh, yes, it's not that. And it's not that he's too young for me or that it's too soon or too ridiculous. I confess Razor fits my life. It surprised me, but he does."

"Well?"

"Well, I .... What's that funny smell? Do you smell smoke? Is something burning in the kitchen?"

Tim got up and went inside.

"Fire! Fire! Mother, quickly, there's a fire! Call for help! It's coming from upstairs. I'm going for Liz!"

I went inside, and the kitchen was filling fast with smoke from the hallway. Grace appeared and ran to the door, which I'd left open. She was safe on the screened porch for the moment.

Mattie and several others ran across the lawn toward the house. "We see smoke! We see smoke upstairs! What's happening!"

"I've called 911, but no one must go upstairs or even inside. The fire is moving fast! Tim has gone for Elizabeth. She's in their bedroom!"

Waiting during an emergency heightens the drama and the fear. Time stands still. Suspense is the devil's desire, and Tim did not immediately come back. I was terrified. I called into the thickening smoke, like yelling at a shadow. We all waited outside, and the cat scurried off to find safe cover. Finally Tim appeared, carrying Elizabeth. She looked to be unconscious. Smoke followed them like a menacing stalker.

The fire licked its way through the house, tumbling down the stairs and popping out windows like exploding party favors. Whimsy Towers was made of wood, an easy victim of the ravening creature that surged through its rooms and climbed the walls. A large section of the house began to collapse as the fire engines arrived, sirens screaming. The tower over my bedroom began to tilt; flames billowed high over the roof.

I stood and watched as if Theodosia were at my side and we were watching her dream go up in flames. The fire raged like a devouring villain without mercy.

I felt suspended in time, part of the dream, willing to let go and uncertain of holding on. My mind was confused and fought for survival. Powerful streams of water began to rain down and drench my world. Daylight was slipping into dusk. I sank into the grass and felt Mattie's arm around me.

"We'll be all right. We'll be all right," she kept repeating.

Elizabeth was safely out of the house, and I could see her scorched clothes as Tim began carefully to unwrap the blanket he had carried her in. He put his face close to hers, whispering through his tears. An ambulance arrived, and she and Tim were carried off with flashing lights and no goodbye.

೮

I do not know exactly the next order of events.

Mattie did not leave my side.

I felt wet grass on my face and arms.

Someone covered me with tablecloths.

The wind picked up and carried embers far across the grass.

I called out for David.

೮

"Mother, I'm here! Speak to me, Mother. Can you hear me? It's Kev. Let's get you up off the ground."

There was terror in his eyes, and my son from the day of celebration looked as though he'd been assigned another face, drained of life and color. Other men helped him lift me to a lawn chair not looking towards the house. They stood like sentinels, shielding me from the crackling, soaked inferno, the bonfire of memories.

Somebody handed me a drink that was warm in my hand. It was Joseph. He had smelled the smoke and seen the sky light up with fire. He came running and brought back drinks and warm muffins.

In another hour, it was over. Firemen in heavy suits doused the last bits of blackened timber, and Whimsy Towers was left a partial skeleton of itself.

"What can I do?" Kev asked Mattie. "What shall we do?"

"You will stay with me," answered Joseph. "There is lots of room, and you are most welcome."

"That's so kind," said Kev, as he introduced himself properly to our neighbor. "You are a lifesaver. I think my mother needs to get away from here. I'm so grateful that she's all right."

"Thank you, Joseph," I muttered, feeling dazed and absent.

"How did you know about the fire?" Mattie asked Kev.

"I work with several of these servers at the restaurant. They called me. Brad wanted to come, but we felt it was not a good idea to bring Charlie."

A buzz of strategy swirled between the decision makers, and I sat quietly in the dénouement of a plan out of my control. I did not like feeling powerless.

Who spoke with the police, thanked the firemen, and secured what was left of my house I do not know. I remember being carried along the beach like a child held in strong arms.

I woke up briefly in an unfamiliar bedroom. Some of my clothes lay on a chair. A small bedside light was on, and I could see wallpaper of yellow flowers clustered in huge bunches tied with blue ribbon. I imagined Razor's head on the pillow next to mine, and I cried myself back to sleep.

It was still dark when I awoke again to the sound of loud pounding, insistent banging from outside the house. A male voice was calling for Joseph. I could not quite pull myself awake and rolled over into the comfort of soft sheets.

I dreamed that Razor had come back, that he was trying to talk to me. I felt his touch, his hand on my arm. My body shook gently, and I slowly realized that Razor was sitting on the edge of my bed. He slid in next to me, still clothed, and wrapped his arms around me.

"Razor, I ...."

"Shh, I'm here," he said. "I'm here. That's enough for now."

Chapter Twenty-Six

I woke up resolved. A day of cleansing lay ahead. The first words I heard the morning after my emotional and structural life went up in smoke were, "Are you hurt anywhere, Theresa? I was so scared."

"How did you know?" I asked, realizing I did not have an apparition next to me.

"I was about halfway home when Brad called. I didn't answer the phone while I was driving, but he kept calling. It was getting late, and I finally pulled over. When he told me that Kev had already left, I just turned the car around."

"Please don't leave me again."

Razor looked at me with questions in his eyes but did not speak.

"I do not want to leave this bed until I've told you all the truth. You may hate me, but you'll know what's in store if you stay. Either way, thank you for coming back. I want to have this conversation first and then find out about Tim and Elizabeth. I don't know if Kev spent the night here last night, but I guess you'll either come with me to the hospital or say goodbye again."

We settled into the pillows of the big, four-poster bed, and I began: "You know the story of my inheriting Whimsy Towers, the deaths of my mother and grandmother, Stormy, and the uncertainty of my marriage. It is true that Kevin and I were unable to produce a child. I recklessly didn't consider if I could conceive with another man. I didn't expect to be unfaithful, was not looking for it, but Rick and I fell into each other's lives. We tried to stop but could not. I'm sure he is the father of my three boys. Each was conceived in the summer. Kevin was finally willing to consider adoption, but when I became pregnant with Tim, he accepted the wonderful news."

"He wasn't suspicious?"

"I think being eager and grateful may dull one's reason, and he'd never had occasion to question my fidelity. If he suspected, he never brought it up. The boys could easily be Kevin's, if you don't see them next to Rick or have any reason to wonder."

"How could you continue the deception?"

"Razor, I am not proud of this story. I was young, infatuated, a little rebellious, yet still loyal to Kevin in my own way. I lived with him, slept with him, and I loved him. We had three wonderful children, a family that would have been denied us. I chose Kevin and not Rick."

"And Rick has never known the truth about the boys? That's incredible."

"No, and when he decided to marry, we stopped the physical contact. I'm sure he's never been unfaithful to his wife, and as you've seen, our families have been good friends. Kevin and Rick were good friends."

Razor sat perfectly still, processing a history of secrets outside his normal cases of intrigue.

"And there's more," I said, taking a deep breath, "the worst and most horrible part. I can hardly tell it."

I began to shake as tears formed, and Razor put his arm around me.

"Take your time."

"Oh, Razor, I cannot bear to remember. It is the worst possible thing in the world, a deed so unspeakable." I gazed in silence at the flowers on the wallpaper and then began: "You know from the dinner after David's funeral that he wanted to marry Susan, Rick's daughter. He obviously didn't know that she was really his sister, his half sister. I tried to get him to wait, to reconsider. I was looking for time, hoping for a miracle that would cancel what seemed a wonderful idea to everyone. At the subway in New York, we argued, and I ... I .... Razor, I pushed him, and he fell in front of the subway car. I didn't actually remember what had happened until later, but I pushed him; I killed my child. I should be in prison. Now you know the whole, terrible truth."

I sobbed into Razor's shoulder as he held me.

A tap on the door was Mattie asking if we wanted coffee.

"Thanks, Mattie, we'll come down in a few minutes," Razor responded. His voice was kind. "Theresa, I thank you for leveling with me. I've had enough secrets in my profession to know I don't want them close to me. I need to sort out the paternity issue, but I want to tell you something about David's death."

"What can you know about that?"

"It's what I do. I was curious about how a grown man, of stable mind, could fall in front of a moving subway car. They have very sophisticated cameras in the New York subway stations, and I know people who allowed me access to the day David died."

"What?" I said, sitting up straight.

"Theresa, you did not kill him. Listen to me, you did not do it."

"But I pushed him; I pushed him."

"Yes, you did. You clearly pushed him. The film is unambiguous on that point. You were arguing and were both engaged, distracted. But you did not notice that David was being set up by two pickpockets. It's clear on the film. As you pushed him, and not that hard, one of the men was reaching for David's trouser pocket. The jolt caused him to grab at David, which spun him around on the platform and into the path of the train. These men work in pairs, and as the one got his hand stuck in David's pocket as they staggered, they pivoted in a way, and David is the one who got thrown. Your push unsteadied him, and them, but was not the fatal cause. He was pushed in front of that train by a local thug trying to save himself. Believe me, I've watched the whole thing many times. I'm so very sorry."

"I don't know what to say."

"I didn't see the need to tell you, because, of course, I had no idea you felt responsible. I didn't want to add details to the accident. I brought in some experts, and we tried hard to identify the two men. They both wore hoodies. Law enforcement are still on the case. I think it helped to have some pressure from people at higher security levels! Petty crime doesn't usually attract heavy hitters from out of state, especially from Washington, D.C."

An enormous load began to lift. "Razor, you've changed my whole world, again."

"I'm so sorry you've been carrying that burden, Theresa. The death is already too much to bear; you must release the responsibility. It truly was an accident, a horrible, senseless accident."

I sat still for several minutes.

"Can you forgive me about the boys?"

He kissed my forehead and said, "They were not an accident. Let's have breakfast and review the options."

"How about a shower first?" I answered.

For those who have not tried it, the most sensual pleasure possible is having a shower with someone you love, washing his or her hair, feeling slippery bodies and the desire brought on by hands spreading warm soap suds. Youth adds agility to this experience, but age is not an obstacle to intimacy. We emerged clean and, well, clean.

The kitchen smelled of bacon and coffee and Joseph's famous cinnamon buns. We entered and saw that Kev had also spent the night.

"Joseph, I cannot thank you enough for your help. I don't know how I can ever repay your kindness."

Joseph looked at Mattie and smiled. "It's my great pleasure, and you are all welcome here as long as necessary. It's good to have people in the house. I called the owners this morning, and they're very glad you are safely here."

"And thanks again for letting me in when I nearly banged down your door in the night! I was a little frantic," added Razor.

Everyone smiled at the only two people in the room with wet hair.

"Kev, have you talked to the hospital this morning?" I asked.

"Yes, and we can go by any time this morning. I actually was there quite awhile last night, but I wanted you to sleep. Tim has some burns on his hands and arms, and his hair is singed. He can probably leave today. Elizabeth is in much more serious shape. They found excessive alcohol in her system, so she had probably passed out. If Tim had not found her, she would never have gotten out. Large areas of her body have been burned."

"I don't want to see the house this morning, if no one minds. I'd like to go straight to the hospital."

"Razor, are you in?" asked Kev. "We can take two cars, and I'll continue on home."

"I'm in," he replied, not looking at me.

We had breakfast at the kitchen table, sitting in sunshine, sharing our recollections of the night before and considering possibilities for going forward. No one knew if the house was salvageable, and no one knew what had caused the fire.

Going out the front door enabled us to see more of the grand house we had slept in: the music room, complete with a harp; billiards room; a smoking room where mounted wild animal heads peered down from the walls; and a room so pink and feminine that it felt like stepping into a rose blossom. The main hall was lined with large portraits in gilded frames, men and women from other centuries with stern faces looking straight ahead, frozen in lace collars or stiff jackets. It was an eerie gauntlet to run. Perhaps ghosts don't rise up if the ancestors are keeping watch.

Kev took my arm on the steps and began to walk me toward Razor's car.

"Shall I go with you?" I asked.

"No, Mother. You and Razor need to work this out. He left here a melancholy man yesterday. I don't know what the problem is. Neither of you is being honest with Brad and me, but we hope you can resolve it. Please don't lose something wonderful."

Love disarms. Kevin Jr. had cut right to the bone.

"Looks like I'm your passenger, if that's all right. My son has done the seating arrangements."

Razor laughed as the doors closed. "I think we are safe together."

"Razor, I was afraid that if you knew how broken I was, you would not love me. Perhaps holding on to my secrets was instead a cry to reveal them. Thank you for listening so patiently and especially for the revelation about David's death. I've carried that horrible guilt so long and still feel partly to blame, but I understand the bigger picture. It doesn't change the outcome, but I understand. I do still have regrets and mistakes."

He looked at me before starting the engine. "Theresa, we can't have a relationship based on an ideal vision, on something perfect. That is fantasy and assumes that no one has a past. We are products of what has gone before, of how our principles have been made evident in our lives. There is success and failure in that. It's called being human. I'm respectful of your freedom. I love your independence."

"Is there a 'but' in this train of thought?"

"You confirmed what I had already worked out. Which do you think is worse, the truth or the fact that you wouldn't tell me?"

I felt appropriately chastised.

He started the car, and we pulled behind Kev, riding in silence for a few moments.

"What shall I do?" I asked.

"Theresa, I don't want to diminish in any way your boys' relationship with their father."

"And telling them the truth would not do that?"

"I confess I honestly do not know. They were Kevin's sons. He loved them unconditionally, and they him. They were more than sperm donations that allowed for a family; they were the fulfillment of a desire that was honest and hopeful. I'm not sure I see purpose in shattering that." He continued to stare ahead at the road. "It was your unwillingness to confide in me. It put a wall up."

"I understand, and I don't blame you. You know I did give birth to each of those boys! I've watched through the years for hints of paternity. And the funny thing is, I've always felt that Kev was the least like Rick. He is the son who got his father's name, and it would be a marvel of science if, in fact, he was Kevin's own child."

We pulled into the hospital parking lot, and Razor turned off the car.

"Where do we go from here?" he asked.

"That's rather up to you. I'd like to wake up every day with you next to me. I have long since worn out my youthful indiscretions. As far as the boys, the family bloodline, if there were one, has halted with Kev and Tim in this generation. And you may like to know that Rick is probably moving to Germany to be with his wife. Shall I try to make you jealous by telling you that he came over yesterday and wanted us to give romance and life together another try?"

"Consider me jealous," Razor answered, leaning over and kissing me.

Kev was standing at the door, smiling.

"Well, that's more like it," he said. "Was the road to the hospital long enough?"

"I won't ask 'long enough' for what!" I answered.

ೞ

Tim was released from the hospital that morning. Elizabeth remained for many more weeks. She had difficult operations that involved skin grafting, but she was strong and determined, and Tim spent every day with her.

Whimsy Towers was not a total loss. The fire had begun with a cigarette dropped by Elizabeth in their bedroom. Investigators found a nearly empty bottle of bourbon next to the charred bed.

It was decided that Tim and Elizabeth would take over Whimsy Towers and make it their home. Tim's interest in architecture has led him into building and house restoration on the Cape. They did not have children, but Elizabeth has become a tireless volunteer for stray and abandoned animals, including endangered species. Countless fundraiser events and programs have been held at Whimsy Towers, giving it life. Theodosia would like that. Liz has many scars from the fire that she says are just a reminder of the past. Her long road of recovery provided time and support to also finally get sober. She's never had another drink.

Kev and Brad adopted two more children, siblings who had been abandoned in Boston. They hired a live-in nanny.

And Mattie? Yes, she married Joseph. They stayed awhile in the big house on the beach and then started their own small bed and breakfast in Chatham, where they are well-known for their baked goods.

Razor and I are inseparable. We talk of marriage but enjoy still choosing each day to be together. We divide our time between St. Michaels, where Razor has stayed active at the maritime museum, and in a small cottage on the water in Provincetown. My children's books are selling well, and I get to read them to my grandchildren. Getting old does not mean getting more needy. We practice gratitude. I am no longer reluctant and fearful about the future. Every night I fall asleep in love. I don't even know where I left my cane.

Acknowledgments

"Richard Cory"
  Edwin Arlington Robinson

"Sonnets from the Portuguese"
  Elizabeth Barrett Browning

Ecclesiastes 3:1-8
  King James Bible

"Abide with Me"
  Henry Francis Lyte

"To Althea, from Prison"
  (excerpt)
  Richard Lovelace

"To the Virgins, to Make Much of Time"
  Robert Herrick

"Amazing Grace"
  John Newton

"The Rubaiyat of Omar Khayyam," V: 71
  (excerpt)
  Edward Fitzgerald

"Roll, Jordan, Roll"
    Slave spiritual,
    adapted from Charles Wesley

"Dover Beach"
    (excerpt)
    Matthew Arnold

About the Author

CREDIT: Robert C. Arnold

Ann Hymes is a retired real estate broker and the mother of two grown daughters. She has a B.A. in English from Mills College and an M.A. in English from Washington College. Her published work includes creative nonfiction. *Love & Lies* is the sequel to her novel *Shadow of Whimsy: A Cape Cod Love Story.* An active international volunteer who served in the Peace Corps, Ann lives in Laguna Hills, California.

She can be reached at *whimsytowers@gmail.com.*

Printed in the USA
CPSIA information can be obtained
at www.ICGtesting.com
LVHW041734211023
761754LV00032B/904/J